Three Days in the Pink Tower

Three Days in the Pink Tower

EV KNIGHT

Creature Publishing
Brooklyn, NY

ISBN 978-1-951971-07-6
LCCN 2022933520

Cover design by hortasar
Tarot card illustrations by Brad Gischia
Spine illustration by Rachel Kelli

CREATUREHORROR.COM

🐦 @creaturelit

📷 @creaturepublishing

For all the women who have drawn the tower card.

CONTENTS

"Tarot is storytelling. It's what we do when we read the cards. Telling stories imbues us with supernatural power—the power to change our story."

—Sasha Graham, *The Magic of Tarot: Your Guide to Intuitive Readings, Rituals, and Spells*

Author's Note

On June 26th, 1992 at 2:59 p.m. on a Friday afternoon, I was a normal seventeen-year-old girl with my whole future ahead of me. It was the summer before my senior year of high school, I had a great set of friends—three of whom I considered my *best* friends—and a boyfriend with whom I had just celebrated three years. The way I saw things, I would be graduating and going to Penn State University, majoring in Biology/Pre-Med. My boyfriend would, of course, go there too for pharmacy school. We'd be married, successful people with 2.5 kids, a dog and a summer house somewhere in Florida.

At 3:00 p.m., my doorbell rang and everything changed. The story you are about to read is based on that moment in my life—on the "incident" that took away that future, that altered me in such a way that now, thirty years later, I'm just beginning to see the ghost of the girl I once was peeking through the protective walls I built around my soul.

When I decided to write this novella, I wasn't sure where I'd go with it, or how I would tell my story. I started by just hauling all my old files out and reading through them, opening myself up to the old sharp details that time has worn down like river stones and found that some are still quite pointy. I put a request in to the Pennsylvania State Police through the Freedom of Information Act for copies of my statements, my attackers' statements, etc. I waited for three months before I got the "sorry you can't have access to any of this. It's not for public consumption" response. *Whatever.* I have typewritten copies of all my statements anyway. That is to say, a lot of the dialogue in this novella is verbatim to what was actually said—or at least what I reported the following day to have been said.

So, I had all these facts, but what to do with them? I could write a memoir, I supposed. But for what? That's just another way for me to say #metoo. Why does *my* story matter? Plus, frankly, after thirty years, I'm pretty goddamned sick of it. Fuck that story, fuck those guys. Fuck getting on the stand and being questioned about my sex life, what I was wearing at the time, why I didn't try to jump out the unlocked door of a moving car. Why didn't I just "take a bite out of crime" when he was forcing my head down on his dick with one hand, while pointing a gun at me with the other?

You think I'm kidding? I'm not. And I was "lucky" because my rape wasn't a date rape, wasn't a result of some drunken frat boy taking advantage of me being too passed out to put up a fight. My rapists walked into my home, pulled a gun, and took me away. Seems pretty cut-and-dry, right? How could anyone question that I was, in fact, a victim? I don't know—ask their defense attorneys.

Clearly, the whole vicious victimization cycle women go through just to get some justice is vomit—if not murderous rage—inducing. I used that rage to retell my narrative, to use my craft as a fiction writer to take back all the control of *MY* story. Because that's the power I have inside me, a power they could not take away. They gave me a real shitty gift, so I upcycled it. That's why this novella and others like it are important to share. I want women to read this and know that no one can take your story from you. It is yours, and you can do whatever you want with it. You can tattoo it, you can cover it with graffiti—hell, you can write the whole thing out, set it on fire and dance naked around it while drinking Everclear! But whatever you do, get it out of you, and take back control.

At the time I wrote this (and still today), I'd been dabbling in the Tarot, and in the idea that the Universe has your back and sends you signs. I truly believe that. I'd recently read Sasha Graham's book *The Magic of Tarot: Your Guide to Intuitive Readings, Rituals, and Spells*. I decided to use the Tarot in my retelling. I could send my younger self a message through it. I—as the creator and not the victim— could represent The Universe in "Josey's" world. With that mighty realization came the understanding that I controlled the ending as well. This novella is the mixed media inspiration for everyone who has survived trauma. It is my way of giving you permission to take it all back and do whatever you want with it.

I am the High Priestess of my past; I am the Creator.

Say that with me now: *I am the High Priestess of my past; I am the Creator.*

Good, feel that power?

Wield it.

The Querent

Thursday, June 25th, 1992

THE HANGED WOMAN

I.

I'm alone in the dark.

I don't know where my friends are or how a cheap carnival "fun house" could possibly be this pitch black. It's cold and damp like a cave. I tell myself the humidity explains the goosebumps and the hairs on the back of my neck standing at attention, and I assure myself I'm not afraid to be wandering around lost in this finite maze. I mean it *is* finite and there were a lot of people in line behind us. I'll run into someone eventually. I'm not going to yell out to Katie or Angie—I'd never live the embarrassment down.

But where are the lights and the mirrors? Where's the fog machine? I can't even smell it anymore. Earthy, dusty air brings my mind to my grandmother's dirt cellar where, I used to believe, the trolls from fairy tales would lay in wait for a little girl sent to grab a jar of beans.

I gotta shake this off. I'm seventeen; I'm about to be a senior. I'm not going to be afraid of this stupid two ticket "attraction." I find the wall—kinda sticky, and I have to force the thought of some fungal layer of ooze out of my head—and follow it. Filmy fingers brush at my hair and I do the 'a bee is trying to get me' kung-fu. Uck, I hate this. Where is everyone?

There's a door—I can feel the edge. My finger follows the groove upward—on my tiptoes—to the top and across. No knob. I push it, but nothing happens—I try the other side, and it springs, swinging just enough toward me that I can wriggle my hand in to pry it open it all the way. Orange light, just dim enough to allow my pupils to adjust without blinding me, lights the small dorm-sized space. *This is definitely not part of the fun house.*

Before I can take in much more than a small cot, a lamp, and a lawn chair, a man—overweight, greasy, and shirtless—leans into view.

"What the fuck?"

"Oh, I'm . . . uh . . . I'm sorry. I got turned around." As I speak, I watch his eyes scan my body. The corner of his mouth twitches into a smirk and then falls back to its previous irritated baseline. A tongue, sprinkled with bits of chewing tobacco, slides out between his lips as he wets them, leaving one shred of dark fiber behind before it retreats again.

"Nah, sweetheart, you're good. You want to come in?"

I don't. I step back and put my hands up as he steps to the threshold of the door and then beyond it. "It's pretty dark back this way," he adds. The door closes, and we're plunged back into the darkness . . . only now I am not alone.

I run. I make last second decisions whether to turn right, left, or keep going straight and am rewarded in my chaos by light. Then I slam into a window. Beyond it, I can see Ang, Katie, and Danielle outside the building. They are looking inside, craning their necks to watch for me. I bang on the glass but get no response. Danielle is checking her watch. She probably has to be home early so she can teach Vacation Bible School tomorrow.

Instead of my usual irritation at her devotion to church, I feel the need to be saved myself. Whatever I did to deserve this probably has a little something to do with my recent agnosticism. How far back is the guy from the dingy room? Would he come after me all the way here, where he could be seen?

I'm about to hit the glass again when a hand grips my upper arm and jerks me backward. I scream and swing my free arm out.

"Hey!" Ang says letting go of my arm and shoving me outside. "What the hell, Jos?"

I squint in the summer sun at my friends who look back at me with a combination of humor, confusion, and concern.

"Oh shit, I thought you were someone else. I didn't know it was you," I say.

"What were you doing in there for so long? Did you get lost?" Katie reaches out and picks something out of my hair. "You're covered in spider webs. Where were you?"

I run my hands through my hair, ripping at the webs and shaking my surly blonde tresses to ensure no stowaway spiders. "I took a wrong turn down some hall—" I start to say, before Angie interrupts.

"She was mesmerized by her own beauty. I found her staring at herself in the mirror." She laughs, so I do, too, because I feel really stupid. Besides, I didn't see myself at all—I saw them. I must not have realized the door to leave was right behind me, so instead, I banged on a freaking mirror like a dummy. I decide not to tell them about the pervert chasing me. I decide to drop the whole thing then and there. *I'm cool. I can laugh at myself. I'm not at all insecure.*

"I was just pleasantly surprised to see how good one of us looked tonight, that's all," I say and laugh. It's a fake laugh, but it's enough to put a period at the end of the fun house incident, and we move on.

"Well, what should we do now?" Ang asks.

"We should totally check out the bumper cars," Katie suggests. "There might be guys from North Adrian there, or even better, Central."

"It's way too early." It's true, but I mostly say it because I'm not in the right headspace for flirting. "There's still just a bunch of kids and their dads there. Later."

She nods.

"Whatever we're gonna do, we should do it now though. I told Mom I'd be home by nine. I'm teaching VBS this week, so I have to be up early," Danielle says.

I knew it. She lives and breathes church. The other two are good churchgoing girls too. In fact, I'm the only one out of the four of us who isn't actively involved in a church youth group. This fact weighs on me a bit, I admit. But right now it doesn't matter, 'cause at the moment, besides Danielle, we're like most average teens given a small breath of freedom—God and the Bible aren't high on anyone's list of priorities.

"I don't care what we do, except can we *please* get away from this Matterhorn? It's so loud!" Grandma Danielle puts her hands over her ears to accentuate her dramatic complaint.

Angie comes up behind Danielle and grabs her arms, flailing them out while singing along with Aerosmith's "Rag Doll" playing loudly behind us. We laugh and move on. After another few feet, a different sound steps up to the mic—the calliope of the carousel. It's weird how many different songs are playing at once, punctuated by the game barkers and screams from the fast rides. The cacophony is only one arm of assault to the senses, though, as a myriad of smells waft along on the breeze. Fried foods, hot sausages, cotton candy and funnel cake compete with horse manure, carny sweat, cigarette smoke, and occasionally, pot smoke. I read once that dogs' noses are like a hundred-thousand times better than ours. You want to see a dog go nuts? Bring 'em to the carnival!

My nose, nowhere near as good as a canine's, smells French fries, and my stomach lurches.

"You guys wanna eat now? That way, we aren't hungry later when it's time for rides . . . "

"Oh my god, yes!" Katie yells and takes off running like a weirdo. I look to see if anyone is watching. No one seems to care, so I do an exaggerated skip over to her and the others follow. I envy Katie. She doesn't care what other people think when she acts silly in public. She's so smart, and she's in a lot of extracurricular activities, so she is pretty self-assured. I can't do that; I have to help take care of my brothers. Katie is cute with her curly red hair and short stature. And she is seriously the nicest person in the world.

"Share a large?" I ask them.

"Yum!" Danielle says.

"Salt and malt?" Because who doesn't want malt vinegar on carnival fries?

"Gross. Not me," Angie says. "You guys enjoy. I'll get something else." Now, Ang is different. She too is super confident. She's that pretty, girl next door kind of brunette. Never looks like she tries hard, and she is a total tomboy. Guys love her. They flock to her because she challenges them. She plays trombone, she hunts—she's just not afraid of anything.

"More for us then," Katie says with a shrug.

Katie, Danielle, and I are scarfing our fries at a picnic table beside a trashcan that smells like vomit when Angie plops down with a corn dog and cup of cheese sauce.

"They had cheese sauce?" Katie whines, and we realize our fatal error.

Every teenage girl knows, if cheese sauce is available, it goes on everything. Suddenly, the vinegar tastes like sour grapes. We eat all the fries anyway, vomit-garbage and cheese-envy be damned.

The food helps to clear my mind. Suddenly, the stuff at the fun house seems to have happened to someone else, a long time ago. I feel like me again. Ready to get out there and be someone else for a night. The best thing about the summer street carnival is that it attracts boys from all over. High school status means nothing.

I check out the bumper cars—still too many kids. The chance of getting bumped by a hot guy is much too low. Our best shot is on the cool rides like the Gravitron and the Matterhorn, but those are bad ideas with a full stomach, unless we want to walk around the rest of the night wearing *eau d'regurge* perfume. Not sexy at all.

Later, then, after Danielle is gone. It's hard to flirt properly when she's around anyway—she's always judging. So what if I have a boyfriend? It's harmless. We only pick boys from other schools who don't know us.

It's like this: I'm not popular, I'll readily admit that. I'm not rich—not by a long shot. I'm the eldest daughter of a thrice-married, once-widowed, twice-divorced single mother. I don't wear designer clothes but I try to dress as fashionably as I can. Basically, I'm just good enough to fly in the safety zone between preps and losers. My only competition is within my small bubble of friends, and Danielle doesn't really compete. Danielle is gangly, tall, and goofy but never outlandish. She is, as I said, a child of God. She is perfectly fine in that role. She and I are the two blondes in our Charlie's Angels quartet, but I'm for sure the one that has more fun.

Sometimes I wonder, if given the chance to cheat on Greg, would I? I like attention from boys. What I lack in brand-name clothes, I make up for in outfits that accentuate my curves (of which I have the most of all of us). I hate that I need outside validation, but I do. I like it, and I want it.

Just not from creepy carnival guys lurking in some rape room in a fun house. I scrunch my nose at the thought and shake it out of my head.

Behind us, broken by the obnoxious calls of the game barker—a greasy, toothless wonder in a trucker hat— the tinkling tune of "Itsy-Bitsy Spider" flows from the megaphone-looking speakers in the corners of the game booth. There're some older boys playing the game—they sit on stools and aim water pistols at silver pipes decorated with giant painted spiders. If you aim your water just right, and it goes straight into the hole, your spider climbs to the top. The first one there wins a prize.

I watch, entranced. The spiders are big and hairy with red eyes. I'm not afraid of spiders, but I'm not a big fan of them either, especially when they and their webs take up residence in my hair. Of the four of us, I'm the big horror fan. I read Stephen King and Dean Koontz like they're going out of style. I've read about plenty of menacing spiders. But these arachnids—I can't decide if I'm amused or creeped out by them.

I don't know that I intend to approach them until I find myself standing at one of three empty seats mid-game. The spider on that pipe has no hope of making it up the water spout, yet it's still wiggling back and forth, ready to go.

I feel like there is a spider crawling up the back of my neck. Involuntary chills roll through me, and I flip my hair away from my neck.

"Let's play!" Angie jumps up on a stool and plops her money down, making me jump back and blink. The imagined spider has left my scalp and waits motionless at the bottom of the pipe. Danielle and Katie hesitate—they're still sipping on their "hand-shaken" lemonades which likely came out of a powder tin. I've never been one for citrus-flavored drinks.

For me, it isn't about competing with boys. No, I need to vanquish the echoes from the dark, web-coated hallway from my head. I sit down on the stool directly across from the most menacing spider of the bunch. If I don't do this, and then I go home to an empty house, I'll be sleeping with the light on and a knife under my pillow. *Why do I read that horror shit when it always does this to me? Why can't I read romances like normal girls?*

"Because you know that monsters are real, Josey," the big spider says. Her voice sounds ancient and raspy. "Because when you read those things, somewhere, in the back of your mind, you keep the stories. All of them—even those creepy fairy tales your grandma used to read to you. You keep the knowledge of things unseen, of things in the woods, and in the darkness—because that knowledge might keep you alive. You know what's out there waiting, Josey, and don't you dare forget it."

No one else acknowledges the strangeness of this. No one else seems to care that this garish red-eyed monstrosity is quickly becoming the foreshadowing character in some horror book. Everyone else is smiling and laughing.

I pick the gun up. I don't want to hear any more. I need to send this thing back to its hole. The boys stick around, apparently feeling the need to show off in front of Ang and me. But maybe they don't know it's not a game. *This is life or death. Someone—or something—has to die and it ain't gonna be me.*

My hands are shaking, so it takes me a minute to line the stream up into the pipe.

The spider leers. "That's it, Josey. It's okay to be scared, but you have to fight. You can't let the monsters eat you up."

I try to ignore her words. I *like* horror. I'm not afraid of monsters. I'm not 'little Josey' anymore.

I don't blink again until my spider reaches the top of the pipe, and only then because the brood has returned. When my spider reached the top, a green light and siren go off. The cacophony silences the spider's telepathic messages.

While I glare at it, daring her to say just one more thing to me, I realize everyone on the stools is staring at me. I loosen my finger from the trigger and put the gun down. *I win.* I ignore the looks because they can't possibly understand the terror I've experienced today. Instead, I point to the single black stuffed dog hanging among others sewn from the same pattern but in brighter colors—pinks, blues, yellows, greens. He is the only one of his kind. The only one even remotely realistic, which is why it *must* be him. He can sniff out trouble; his senses are thousands of times better than mine.

The slimy-looking carny gives me a look as if I somehow snuck a goth version of his prizes up there myself, but he hands it over just the same. His fingers brush my hand. They're cold and damp. He's grinning, and I realize that, as I lean across the counter for my puppy, I've given him a good view of my cleavage. I clutch the prize in my arms like a toddler, and my knees go a little weak. Maybe he's the monster and I should run away? Maybe I should. Except, I'm exhausted. I want to drop to the ground and cry in a fetal position until someone comes along, picks up my tired body, and carries me to the car.

"Nice shootin', Tex." One of the boys pats me on the back and then pets my dog on the head as if it's real. "He looks like he belongs to you. You guys are perfect for each other!"

It makes me smile, and my terror dissipates as quickly as it came. I'm me again. All grown up.

"Turns out I just really hate creepy crawlies!" I shrug.

"You guys hear that? She doesn't like creeps—I'd be on my best behavior, if I were you."

We all laugh, and just like that, our two groups become one. Brian, 'my guy,' introduces his friends—Aaron and Kris. It always seems in groups of multiple guys and girls, inevitably, they somehow just naturally pair up. Aaron and Katie, Kris and Ang. Danielle is the odd one out, which doesn't make sense, as I have a boyfriend, but Brian made his choice. Who am I to disagree with fate? Is it fate? Is this my chance to find out just how good of a girl I really am? Maybe he's just my safety net for the night, or as long as it takes to erase the awful memories of this night out of my head.

Turns out, it's all harmless flirting anyway—these guys, we discover, are twenty-three! Way too old for us, but that explains Brian's maturity in the face of my strange gameplay. I'm still too absorbed in the oddness of that whole experience. The idea of riding the Gravitron or even the Matterhorn with them seems bad—really bad. I need to clear my brain, not scramble it further. I assure everyone that I will wait nearby and encourage them to go on without me. I might head over to the funnel cake trailer or watch the little kids try to throw ping-pong balls into fish bowls. *I wonder what the world record is for the longest living carnival fish?*

I suddenly feel for the fish. They're always the losers in that game—stuck inside a tiny glass prison, terrified of what is happening beyond their walls. Waiting for the giant ball of doom to land. These fish watched their friends and family be carted off in little plastic baggies. There they will live in their own aquatic version of death row, where some new warden will torture them for a day or two before growing bored and either neglecting them to death or actively killing them. *Poor fishy—I do not envy you.*

A small girl appears out of nowhere, running straight into me. Her dark curls bounce as she throws her hands up to stop herself against my middle. I drop my little black dog and she drops her bouquet of dandelions—likely picked from the ballfield beside the carnival, and probably for her mom.

"Oh no! Are you okay?" I bend over to help her pick up her flowers. She grabs up my stuffed dog and hugs it. When we finally make eye contact, she steps back from me. Her dirty pink t-shirt with a faded Charlotte's Web movie poster, the words "Some Pig" written in the web, is about four sizes too big for her.

"Here," I tell her, trying to put the now-wilted flowers back in her hands. When I touch her, she jumps.

"Run away, run away, run away," the little girl whispers, over and over again like some cultish chant.

"Hey, are you okay?" I ask again, but she turns and follows her own instructions. I follow her, trying not to look like some freak. She weaves in and out of the crowd while I slow walk behind. I feel like Jason from *Friday the 13th* lumbering after the poor kid who is scared of me—*I think*—for some reason.

At the far end of the oval-shaped carnival setup, I see her slip into a canvas tent. There are only a few 'old school' circus-type tents anywhere on the grounds. One held a fake oddities exhibit, which I wasted a buck on last year to see bad fake taxidermy and a man sitting in a chair eating a chicken leg. The sign wasn't a lie, I guess, since "The Incredible Man Eating Chicken!" could be construed as technically accurate. Other than the oddities tent, this is the only other relic—a small, round tent draped in beads and filmy scarves tied corner to corner. The thing looks like one big chrysalis.

Somewhere inside this tent is the little thief who took my prize. The faded hand-painted sign leaning against the tent reads:

Psychic Tarot Reading
$10 for reading
$25 to take home your spread

I try to decide what to do while the noise of the carnival continues around me. Looking around, I see the carny from the spider game lurking about ten feet behind me. He's smoking a cigarette. He might be on his break, but he might be following me just like the other guy.

Run away.

No one is sitting at the table under the umbrella in front of the tent. *How do you knock on canvas?* I decide you don't, and just as I am about to slip inside, a woman comes out. By the looks of her, I assume it's my little friend's mother. Long, dark walnut-colored curls fall to the middle of her back. Her linen palazzo pants are green and spirals have been bleached onto her pants and matching tunic. A scarf, similar to the ones hanging along the tent, pulls her hair away from her face. It's unbelievably perfect. Skin like marble. In fact, she looks like a goddess—one chiseled from stone in ancient Greece come alive. I can't stop staring at her.

"You want a reading." Her husky voice is powerful and deep. It's missing the smoothness of someone her age.

"Uh, I don't know," I stammer. How do I tell her I was chasing her daughter because she stole my dinky stuffed dog prize? "I saw a little girl run in there, and she has—" I hold up the droopy yellow weeds as if trying to explain.

"It wasn't a question," she responds. "Sit." She goes back into the tent so I sit, wondering if this is some gimmick—some mother-daughter trick to bring in customers. When she doesn't return immediately, I begin to feel foolish, duped and exposed. I check the position of the carny but he is gone, back to whatever hole he crawled out of. I'm about to stand and slink away quietly when an old woman steps gingerly out of the tent. She is dressed in complementary fashion to the other two females, but in all black. Her white hair has been braided and rolled into a bun on the top of her head.

But it's not her clothes or her hair that demands my attention, it's her eyes. They are covered in a white film, both of them. I can't see any color beneath the white, but I can see the bulge of her iris and pupil mounded up off the globe. I assume she is blind, but her daughter didn't come out with her, so maybe not? Maybe they're just some weird cataracts? Either way, I need to stop staring.

She finds the empty chair easily and sits with a groan. From somewhere beneath the table or within the folds of her skirts, she produces a black velvet bag which she opens to reveal a pack of well-worn tarot cards. Expertly, she shuffles them. I haven't paid, she hasn't asked me any questions, and I'm almost certain she can't see me. There is nothing keeping me sitting there. I could just sneak away quietly. My friends are probably looking for me.

Yet, at the same time, I'm enthralled. The Tarot, paganism, witchcraft—it all fascinates me. More so since I've (secretly) left religion. I do believe there is *something* out there. The idea that we die and then there is nothing terrifies me. I can't accept that. I've never seen a ghost but I think I want to. I need to believe in something. It's just so hard to explore other options when all my friends and family are religious. Maybe this is my chance? Plus, this whole thing has been so strange—first the game, the carny, and then the girl and her mother, now this old woman who could be a grandmother or even great-grandmother of the adult woman. And where are the mother and child? Are they hiding in the tent, watching me?

"Split the deck into three," the old woman says, and I do.

"Pick the stack you want to work with." I'm not sure what to do, so I tap one. She grasps my hand in her warm, leathery grip and rubs her thumb across the back of my hand. "Hmm. So many questions, so much fear and uncertainty."

I blurt out, "The little girl, the one who ran into your tent? She took my stuffed dog."

She doesn't answer me. Instead, she flips the first card over and runs her hands across the picture of a woman hanging one-legged from a tree.

"The querent card. The Hanged Man."

"Is that bad?" I ask.

"You are searching for spiritual guidance. You do not feel in control. You are young, early in the fool's journey. You face a great test, of yourself and your beliefs. You must balance what you know with the understanding that there is much you do not know. You must be willing to release in order to receive."

"I don't know what that means." *Of course* she says I am looking for spiritual guidance; I'm getting a tarot reading.

She says nothing more. Instead, she deals more cards, stopping to touch each one, running her fingers along the lines of the illustrations as if she can see them perfectly well. As far as I can tell, there is no braille on them.

I read the cards as she deals out my fate: The Tower, Eight of Swords, The High Priestess, Five of Cups, Five of Wands, The Devil, Seven of Wands, and finally, Judgment.

She breathes deep. My heart thuds.

"You are a smart girl. Well-read. You think rationally and are fiercely independent." She pauses.

"Okay, sure." I don't know if I'm supposed to say anything.

She holds a gnarled hand up to stop me. "You're young and naïve. You have much to learn."

She touches the tower card, lingering on it. "There is trouble. A change is coming. It will shake you up, change you. There will be uncertainty, there will be loss, there will be fear. You must let go of your rational side and seek answers from the spirits. Do not let your independence be your doom. Ask for aid. Do not get lost at the crossroads. Do you hear me, child?"

I crumple a little. "Yes, but I don't know what any of it means. I just came here to get my stuffed dog."

The old woman's white, sightless eyes never leave mine. I find myself looking away, staring at her hands or the cards. I know she can't see me but at the same time, it feels as if she can see so much of me—more than anyone else ever has. It's unnerving.

She nods. I'm not sure if she is confirming my thoughts or acknowledging that I want my prize back. "Black dogs, snakes, horses, spiders, owls, deer, even butterflies—all messengers from the spirit world. Listen to them. Watch for them when you are in need."

"So, what's gonna happen to me? Those pictures on the cards. They all look bad."

"There is so much here. I see a victim, imprisoned— maybe by your own negative thoughts? But . . . " She brushes her fingers across the Eight of Swords with a picture of a blindfolded woman, hands tied behind her back and surrounded by swords.

"Hmm." She nods and then touches the High Priestess card. This one looks better, more triumphant. That woman looks badass, in total control. "The voices you hear? Let them guide you. You have drawn The High Priestess. Ask her to guide you. She is all things—maiden, mother, crone. She is balance. Seek her guidance, and you may see your trials through to the end.

"Yeah, but look at these cards. They all look bad. There's The Devil! Why is this all so bad?" This carnival held so much potential for fun when we arrived, but it seems like a million years ago. I'm totally freaked out, and I just want my damn stuffed animal back.

The old woman picks up the Five of Cups and pushes it in front of me. "You see her? See how she focuses on the spilled cups and not the two she has still filled? You see the moon? The moon is trying to guide her to what she has left inside of her. Her strength which she has not lost. You must not lose sight. There will be pain, there will be loss, it may seem overwhelming, but you must accept the help the universe gives you; you must trust in its guidance. Do you understand?"

No. I don't understand. I don't want to understand. I want to forget all about tonight. I want to leave. I stand up. "I'm sorry, this is just messing with my head. I thought this would be fun. I . . . I don't know what I thought but I just—" I'm interrupted.

"Josey! Hey!" Ang is leading a pack of frustrated-appearing friends. "You said you'd wait right there. You gotta quit getting lost!"

I dig out ten dollars from my pocket and put it in the old blind woman's hands.

"Listen, I gotta go. I'm sorry, I just wanted to get my dog back, but it's fine. She can keep it. A ten's all I got; I hope that's okay."

The old woman scrapes my cards into a pile. "Take these and bring them back tomorrow. Come here early, as soon as we open, and don't be late. There is more I must tell you."

I take the cards—a fair exchange for the dog, I guess. "I'll try. My car's not super reliable."

She grabs my wrist with a speed and grip that belies her age. "Come. Come here and bring your cards."

"Okay. Okay. I'll try." I have no idea what else to say to her.

As we walk away, Brian paces himself to walk beside me. "What was that all about? You okay?"

I shrug. "Um, yeah. I think so? Some little girl grabbed my dog and took off into that tent with it. I tried to get it back, but that old lady came out instead and just sort of started reading my tarot cards."

"That's crazy! You shouldn't have paid her anything!" Ang says, overhearing me. "You should actually go talk to the management about that girl. It's probably some big setup they pull to get you there, then start talking before you agree to anything so you feel like you have to pay."

"Yeah, maybe," I answer because I thought the same thing. "She said I should come back tomorrow, and she gave me these." I fan the cards out and everyone gathers around them. It's such a taboo subject for most of us. None of our parents would approve of our considering these 'satanic' things. God, everything these days is satanic—it's crazy. Danielle won't even look, but the rest's morbid curiosities get the best of them.

"Are these, like, mostly good cards? Or bad? Like, some of them don't look so good," Aaron asks.

I consider the cards again. "Well, she started off saying a couple good things about me, but then it got dark really fast. I don't know."

"My mom has a book about tarot cards. You could borrow it, if you want. She's out of town, but I'm sure she wouldn't care," Brian offers.

God, what a nice guy. I'm going to have to tell him I have a boyfriend soon. I can feel my friends' eyes boring into my soul, sending me telepathic messages to do the right thing.

I will . . . later.

"Yeah? Well, my mom would shit a brick if I came home with a book on tarot stuff. Hell, I'll have to hide these under my mattress or something. She'd kick me out if she knew I brought them in her house." I stuff the cards in my jeans pocket.

"Well, we could go to her place right now, and you could look your cards up? Heck, I could even hold on to them for you, pick you up tomorrow, bring you back? I can even meet her with you, if you want, for moral support."

I smile up at him. "That'd be awesome. I'll probably get more info from the book than I did from her."

"So, let's go now." He smiles, and I wish no one was with us. I'd do something bad. But my friends save me from everlasting ruin.

"She promised to ride rides with us tonight, and she is not getting out of it!" Katie says, grabbing me by the arm.

"No worries. Offer stands, whenever you're ready," Brian replies easily.

The guys accompany us on most of the rides; they make the bumper cars way too fun. I almost puke from the Gravitron, but my teenage phobia of embarrassment is strong, so I overcome the urge. What I can't seem to overcome is the persistent feeling of being watched. Brian, if no one else, notices each time I look over my shoulder. The thing is, I don't even know what I'm so paranoid about. Is it the leering carny, the old woman, or something else entirely?

The Matterhorn has a dark tunnel on the far side, so as it goes around, you spend half your time in this laser-lit tunnel. In those few seconds of every rotation, faces flash at me—red-eyed spiders, leering carnies, blind, old women, and creepy little girls. I let out a yip of a scream every time we go into the tunnel part. Only Brian, sitting beside me, knows, but I'm still so embarrassed. I've worked myself into such a state of anxiety, I can't possibly stay one minute longer.

I'm ready to go home. How can I explain this to everyone without sounding mental? I agree to let Brian drive me and make my excuses to Katie, who I'd said I would spend the night with. She gives me a disappointed look and I make eyes at her that I hope express my understanding and convey to her that I really am going to tell him I have a boyfriend. My friends are good. They see and they understand, even if they don't agree with my choice to leave all the fun. Ang and Danielle hug me at the same time. Katie waits to be the last one to say goodbye.

"Please don't do anything with him. He's too old for you, and what about Greg?" she whispers in my ear. I feel a ball growing in my throat. At first it's just ping-pong-sized but rapidly surpasses tennis ball to baseball. I try to speak, but I just squeak. Before letting go she says, "Just please be safe. I'll call you as soon as I get home, and you better answer. Otherwise, I'll make Mom and Dad drive me to your house. Or better yet, I'll call the cops to do it. You don't know him."

She's right—I don't know Brian, but I trust him. Maybe I am naïve. Maybe I'm not so smart, too self-assured. Maybe I am about to make the worst mistake of my life. I feel the tower of my good girl persona start to tilt. If something bad happens to me because of this choice I'm making—I deserve it.

On the ride to Brian's mom's house we make small talk. In the dark of the car, I don't see his hand until I feel it on my thigh. I stiffen. What am I doing? This whole night has been messed up. I got weirdos following me around, spiders talking to me, some creepy old blind lady warns me something bad is going to happen, so what do I do? Jump in a car with a strange guy I don't know agreeing to go to a house with him where I know no one is at home!

Brian catches on to my discomfort and pulls his hand away.

"Hey, I'm sorry. I shouldn't have done that. You've just had a shitty time, and I'm not helping the situation. Just know that I'm a good guy. You can trust me."

That's just what a bad guy would say.

"I know. I just think maybe I'd like to go home. I don't need to look at the book. I'll just try to go back tomorrow and talk to her."

"Look, we're practically there. Let me go grab it for you to borrow. It's the least I can do after acting like a chump."

I agree to take the book home. I'll just have to hide it from mom and give it back tomorrow. With the book as a shield over my lap, we ride home in silence.

At my door, Brian keeps his hands in his pockets.

"Hey, I'm such an idiot. I should never have touched you without asking first. I just really liked you, and I got caught up in imagining us as a couple. I swear, I'm a good guy. Can I make this up to you? Can I take you back to the carnival tomorrow?"

I nod. "Okay. I'm sorry, too. I had a crappy night for the most part, and I'm just not really feeling much like myself. I really would like a ride tomorrow, and I do have to get this book back fast before my mom sees." It's my fault anyway, all of it. I wandered off in the fun house, I let my imagination get carried away with the spider game, I let some crazy tarot lady and her granddaughter dupe me out of ten bucks *and my prize puppy*, and I should have told Brian I had a boyfriend right from the start.

So why am I going to let him pick me up again tomorrow?

Brian asks if he can kiss me on the cheek, and I let him.

Because this is the last night that I'll allow myself to make dumb choices. I will tell him about Greg, I promise myself I will. It's time for me to be the person I pretend to be.

Tomorrow. *Everything will be different tomorrow.*

Day One

Friday, June 26, 1992

II.

Except I haven't magically changed.

Mom's in the shower, so I think it's safe to get the tarot book out and look up my cards. I should probably do this in my room, but the couch is my preferred sitting space. The light from the picture window shines right on the coffee table. I can spread all the cards out and I don't have to hunch over like I would on the bed. I don't have a desk in my bedroom. Just a bed, a dresser, stereo, and a closet. I'm a living-room-home-office-kinda gal.

The Five of Wands is about struggle and conflict. But it seems to be about others as well, so maybe it's just signifying my mom and dad's divorce. Although I have a lot of inner conflict right now too, so who knows? Either way, it's another crappy card.

It's The Devil card that gets me in trouble. Mom comes out, wrapped in a towel and before she can say whatever it is that was so important, she sees the cards and the book.

"Josey! What are you doing?"

"Oh, uh, I found these at the carnival sitting on a table."
I hate that I'm such a decent liar on the fly. "I wanted to see
what they were about. Ang's older sister did a term paper on
the Tarot and she brought us the book to look at."

"I don't want you looking at stuff like that. You know
they were talking about this at work. There's been some
Satan worshippers hanging out, doing rituals and stuff in the
woods. They leave stuff like this for people to find. That's how
they recruit, or God-forbid lure, a pretty, young girl into their
group to be sacrificed. You're exactly what they look for—
pale, blonde, blue-eyed—the perfect virgin for sacrificing.
You need to burn that stuff. I don't want it in my house."

"Oh my god, fine," I say. And shove the cards in my back
pocket. "But I can't burn Michelle's book. I'll give it back to
her tonight. We're going to the carnival again and then maybe
we can do a fire at Ang's and I promise I'll burn them then."

"No, I don't want you going to the carnival again. Not if
you found those things there. It's not safe, we'll go tomorrow
when I'm off."

"Mom! I'm seventeen. I seriously am not going to the
carnival with my mother. Like, for real."

"Well, you're not going tonight either, okay? Just not
tonight. Those Satanists probably saw you pick those up.
They'll be watching for you."

"Okay, fine. I won't go anywhere. I'll sit here at home,
in the middle of nowhere by myself and hope they didn't

follow me home. So, if you come home tonight and I'm dead on an altar in the woods somewhere, it's all your fault." I laugh because this is the silliest thing to worry about and also because if she thought I was serious, I'd probably get my mouth slapped.

I see the anger dissipate and her shoulders slump back to their factory settings. "Maybe I should show you how to work the handgun, just in case." She bought one after she and dad split up. I think it's still in its original box in her nightstand drawer. Unloaded. But hey, if it makes her feel better, who am I to judge?

"No way! I'm not touching that thing. Mom, seriously, relax. Nothing is going to happen."

"I don't like you being here alone. Something could—"

I interrupt. "You're gonna be late for work. I'm fine. Geez."

She opens her mouth to argue but the phone rings, so I jump up to answer. She waits until I say "Hey, Greg" and then heads to her room to dress.

**

I'm still on the phone when she leaves. I stand up to say goodbye and she surprises me with a hug and a kiss on the cheek.

"I love you," she whispers and I nod and mouth 'I love you too.' "Maybe come have dinner with me on my break?" I nod. I know I won't and she won't really expect me to, so it's fine. I walk over to the door and out onto the porch with her. It's hot outside. I can't be out too long or else I'll start to sweat and my permed curls will get frizzy.

Greg is talking about going to a football game with his dad next month and I say all the 'uh huhs' and 'cools' as I wave goodbye to mom.

On the way back inside, I notice that the hummingbirds have come back to the feeder. When did we last fill it with fresh sugar water? Sometimes Mom forgets to change it if they don't eat it all up really fast. With all the rain we've had lately, today is the first sunny day in a while, so it probably needs to be changed. I should do that before I leave.

I sink back onto the overstuffed blue couch across from the picture window. The living room walls are the same color as the sky today; one shade lighter than the couch, so the window seems more like a frame centered in the horizon. The 'picture' within the window's frame shows an unattended yard with grass about a week overgrown, sprinkled with bright yellow dandelions, an ancient oak on the upper left corner, a poplar and pine to the right. From where I sit I can also make out the white steel corner brace of the front porch where the hummingbird feeder hangs. At the very top of the 'frame' runs the old country road. It doesn't have a name like most of my friends' homes. No "Pine Run" or "Pleasant View." Just a route number.

The actual 'art' hangs on the wall above the couch where I sit. It's just a bunch of left-overs from my mother's short stint as an interior décor home party consultant. "For just a few hundred dollars, you could have this entire wall ensemble! We do it for you—there's no thinking involved. You get the painting, the shelf, the wall sconces, the realistic faux flower arrangements, candles, and knick-knacks!"

The paintings are all hideous, and if you wait a season, you can find them at any yard sale in town.

I could lay back on the couch and look up at the underside of a pair of alabaster doves on a denim blue filigree metal shelf if I wanted to, but I just did my hair. I am fully immersed in what I refer to as my mom's 'blue period' of interior design. I can't decide if it's affecting my mood or if my current mood is affecting my distaste for the room.

Greg is talking about practicing with his band this weekend—another excuse not to get together after he worked all week. Maybe we should just break up? One more year of high school, and we'll be off to college . . . what then? But at three years strong, we're the longest running relationship at school—a shoo-in for 'Cutest Couple' in the Senior Who's Who, and probably my only chance to break into that level of local fame. I mean, Who's Who is typically reserved for the popular kids and I shouldn't care what they think, but getting our picture among theirs makes them my peers and it's frankly the only way someone the likes of Josey Claypool could even attain that status.

I decide I'll go for an ice cream after the carnival, see him, say hi, make an effort. We can do one more year together. He's a great guy, and we have so much fun—it's just that we have *only* ever been with each other, and there's a whole world out there.

An expectant pause filled with silent question marks permeates the space between us. In my head, I see them lining up looking at each other all confused as, I suppose, question marks tend to feel, while the seconds tick by.

"Yeah, that sounds good." I hazard a guess at what to say as I tuned out the conversation ages ago.

He sighs. "I asked you what you're gonna do tonight with the house all to yourself."

"Oh, yeah, I'm sorry. I told you about that old blind woman—the fortune teller? She said to come back tonight, because she wanted to talk more, so probably that. She freaked me out with all that talk about my future. Seriously, *none* of the cards were good."

Greg groans, but then says, "I thought you said you got the highest Priest card or something? That's gotta be like the best card, though, right?"

"The High Priestess. And yes, she's cool, but then everything else was kinda bad or, like, sort of menacing." I can't tell him I'm still scared even thinking about it. He'd think I was weak or something—less cool, maybe. Better to keep that bit to myself.

His warm, familiar voice cuts into my thoughts. "Did you consider that this fortune teller does her routine in a way so you'll *want* to come back and pay more money for her to explain this stuff to you? These carnies all have their schtick, ya know?"

He is still talking, but I'm not listening again. I have the cards she pulled in my back pocket. I stand up to get them out again now that Mom's gone, but I'm distracted by a car parked on the side of the road in front of the house. There is a man leaning into the window of the driver's seat talking to someone. I don't recognize the little maroon, four-door hatchback, and I do not recognize the man. *What are they doing?*

He's turning, looking at the house. He points to my car in the driveway and says something else to the driver, and then steps into our yard and walks toward the porch.

"Greg, I gotta go. There's a car out front and some strange guy is headed to the door. I'll call you back in a few."

"I'm leaving for work at four-thirty," he replies.

"Yeah, well, it's three, and this won't take long. I'll call you right back." I don't know why it feels important that I talk to him one more time before he leaves for work, but it does. All of a sudden, I love him again—so much—and I want him with me now.

I watch the guy come up the stairs. He's not very tall, and his steel gray hair is cut in a buzzed, flat-top style. The tint of his hair could be due to dust, as he looks young—mid-twenties, probably. He's chubby and his eyes are bulgy above his stubbled jowls. It's like the nerdy kid from *The Far Side* cartoons is walking through my lawn. Keeping with the cartoonish nature, he is wearing a gray and blue striped t-shirt with a pair of orange gym shorts, no socks, and the grungiest pair of once-white sneakers I have ever seen. The hummingbirds agree and fly off in disgust.

That's the thing about living in the middle of nowhere on a shitty road that they tar and chip a couple times a year instead of just paving. If it isn't a farmer from one of the surrounding fields hopping off his tractor and asking to fill up his water jug, it's some redneck country bumkin in a beat-up car asking to use the phone. Why us? Because we have the only house close enough to the road to see; the rest belong to the farmers and are set way back behind the fields. I often tell my mom we should put out a pay phone and a water vending machine—we'd make a killing.

The doorbell rings. I take a deep breath and open the door.

"Oh, hi there." He leans as if trying to look inside the house. I pull the door close to my body.

"Can I help you?" I try the same maneuver by looking over his shoulder at the man in a ballcap sitting in the car, window down, hand hanging out, tapping out an air beat to music I can't quite hear.

"Is your dad home?"

"My dad doesn't live here." My real dad died in a car accident before I was born. The man I call dad is my second stepfather. If this guy knew my 'dad,' he'd know that. He'd also know my parents have been divorced for a year, and dad lives in a trailer on my uncle's farm just about a mile down the hill from us.

"What about your mom, then? Any older brothers?" There is a gap in his teeth. It's the only part that isn't yellowed with plaque. He could fit a whole 'nother tooth in the space, and I'm trying hard not to stare at it.

"Nope. Can I help you?" I stress this so he stops asking so many stupid questions. *Just tell me. Water or phone? Phone or water? One of each? How can I help you get out of my life?*

He thumbs back at the car. "Out of gas. Can I use your phone?"

Can I interest you in a glass of water as well, sir? "Sure," I say and grab the cordless off the couch.

"Don't worry, I have a phone card."

As if I give a shit.

Eventually, I *do* give a shit because it is taking him forever. He dials, he listens, he dials again. Between dials, he makes stupid confused faces, purses his lips, sticks out his tongue. I stand there with my waiting face, the one that everyone always thinks looks bitchy and makes guys at school and old men everywhere interrupt my thoughts to tell me to smile.

Then he smiles, that gap a black hole in the Yellow Sea. "Maybe I got the wrong number. Can I go talk to my buddy? Make sure I got it right?"

I shrug. "Sure."

I watch him trot back to the car, lean in, say a few a words and then try not to notice his belly jiggling beneath his shirt as he slow jogs—is that even possible? Isn't a slow jog a walk? No, it's a trot, like a stinky, dirty pig. I hate this guy. He is gobbling up the minutes I have to call Greg back before Brian shows up to take me to the carnival. Plus, I haven't put on any lip gloss or reapplied my face powder. It's a hot day.

"Ooh boy, is it ever hot. First hot day though, so I shouldn't complain. Any chance I could get a glass of water?"

Of course. "Did you still need the phone?"

"Oh, uh, yeah, I don't think I had the numbers right, anyway. My buddy's looking for another one now."

I don't like this. I don't like him, and I don't like this. I want it over. I go to the kitchen and fill a glass with tap water and plop in a couple pieces of ice. I don't even wash my hands first. I don't care.

"Nice house," he says. He's followed me inside, an invasive species in my living room threatening to take root if I don't get rid of him soon.

I hand him the glass. He looks me up and down. "You look like you got plans for a hot date tonight. You goin' somewhere?"

As he sips, I start talking. I'm more nervous now. This is not how it typically works. Use the phone, go away. Ask for water, wait on the porch, drink it or take it away. No one stays, no one comes in. He has breached the border and I am alone with a strange man.

"No. No plans," I lie. "Just hanging out here, maybe watch a movie or something. Yeah, the house is nice enough, I guess. My dad built it. We saved a lot of money that way. Contractors built the shell and then—"

He interrupts me. "Hey, do you mind if my buddy comes in for a drink as well? Sure is hot out there, and no AC without the car running."

Oh Lord, what do I even say? *Yeah, sure, what's one more strange man in my house?* I mean what's the worst that can happen? But what are the chances? People do this all the time. The sooner I say yes, the sooner he's gone. So let his buddy have a drink and then they'll leave. Mom's talk about Satanists just has me all worked up, that's all. And the fact that I'm going back to meet with that creepy old lady with her blind eyes that looked like someone covered them with over-easy eggs and a bunch of blood vessels.

Once, my mom cracked open an egg from a dozen we'd bought from a farmer. It was bloody and filled with squirmy-looking vessels and a half-formed chick. Mom gagged, I screamed, and we threw the rest of the eggs out. That old lady's eyes looked like maybe somewhere beneath the white film, deep inside those globes, something was gestating—some mutant embryo waiting to spill out of her. If I go back, will there be blood?

Stop it. It's not her. It's this situation. Snap out of this and get rid of them.

"Sure. Should I get him his own glass?"

"No, he can have some of mine." He steps to the door which is still hanging open and waves his buddy inside.

I watch with nervous anticipation as a taller, thinner man tramples over the dandelions covering our yard, scattering bees with his assault. These men have caused a mass exodus of winged things. Suddenly, I wish I could fly away, too.

This guy has gaps, too, only his are from just flat-out missing teeth. Those left in his skull are not even yellow but gray—they've moved beyond the caution color. He's wearing a red and white trucker hat, but the white part, where *normal people* would have some company logo or sarcastic saying, was blank. As if this guy was filled with blank space. Unlike his friend, he has long hair, a rusty brown color, and it lies slicked against his scrawny neck, trying to curl away but trapped by the viscosity of body oils. His clothes match, though. He is wearing a navy blue t-shirt with some fluorescent design on the side and cut-off jean shorts. To make up for his friend's lack of socks, he has his pulled up to his knees, but they have turned the same dingy color as both of their shoes. This guy is familiar but I can't place why. Something about the way he stands, the way he ogles me and my house.

"Thanks," he says, but he never makes eye contact. He is quiet, as if he would like nothing more than to slither away to the maroon metallic log from whence he came.

"We were just chatting about the house. It's nice, right?" Flat Top says. Slither looks around, up and down, everywhere but at me.

"Yeah." He takes a drink. I see his mustache hairs break the hydrostatic tension of the water's surface. *Gross*. Slither hands Flat Top the glass and thanks me again. He leaves and trudges back to the car, stomping out bright yellow weeds that could have become wishes. I think of the little girl's wilted bouquet and suddenly I want my stuffed dog back really bad.

Flat Top downs the rest of the water, sucking the ice cubes against his liver-colored lips. I open my mouth to offer more, not so much to be nice but to stop the disgusting sound of this slob slurping on *my* glass, *my* ice cubes.

"Do you want to try the phone again?" I ask.

"Oh, yeah, sure. One more time would be great. Thanks." He hands me the glass. I left the phone on the kitchen counter by the sink. I dump the ice in the sink, set the glass down and pick up the phone. It's the last mundane thing I will do.

I turn around with the phone in hand, but before I even realize we're dueling, before I can draw my phone, he's drawn his gun and it is pointing at me. If this were a movie, the camera would do a close-up on the gun—the little black pistol with white sides on the handle. After the viewer got a good look at this deadly weapon, it would track up to the man's face, implying that is the view from my perspective, and it is. It is exactly what I do. Because it takes me a moment to identify this small machine which is actually in use, in the middle of my kitchen, against me. Once I have confirmed that, yes, this is real, I follow the curves of his gut up to his face. Here I am assessing for signs of mirth, signs that this has all been some elaborate joke, and I can, in fact, breathe again.

"You know what this is, don't you?" He isn't that goofy, annoying, dirt ball anymore. Now he is death personified. Death isn't beautiful. Death is filthy and unattractive and unkempt in every way. This is not the death meant for a healthy, youthful girl. This is for perverts, strangers who offer children candy to get into their vans. This is a death for men like my ex-stepfather, who was always drunk and once, in my presence, hit my mom, knocking her to the floor. I want to tell him he has the wrong house. I want to say, *Oh, that dad. No. Mom kicked his ass out. They divorced like twelve years ago. Wish I could tell you where he was though, Sorry.*

I want to run. I want to scream. I want to shove him away from me, grab a knife from the far counter, and slice his damned head off. But the strobe-effect of neural transmissions flashing in reds and yellows, the tannic, bitter taste of adrenaline and the buzz of potential energy in every muscle cell work against each other to paralyze me, to stymie any chance of escape. In this moment, this split second of eternity, I change. I am no longer Josey Claypool, soon-to-be high school senior, applying to pre-med.

No. Now I am just another victim, the pre-dead body of another nameless girl found in a ditch.

I hear a voice say "please don't kill me," and I wonder who it is. Who is the little girl begging him? That little girl was just an echo from the memory of my abusive ex-stepfather. But she grew up, so maybe I just think she said it. My mouth is desert-dry; my stomach seems to be wriggling around in my knees, and it's affecting their ability to keep me upright. My heart is the Cowardly Lion, throwing itself against my rib cage, insisting I let it out so it can run away.

"I just want some money. That's all. We need some money, and we don't want to hurt you."

Why didn't I go to church camp? Suck it up and fake it for one more year? Thank God my brothers did. Is this what the old woman was referring to? If she knew this was going to happen, why would she tell me to come back tonight? Mom. Is she going to find my body tomorrow when she comes home, exhausted from work? Will she think "Damnit, Josey. I told you those Satanists would get you?" *Or will she forget about that whole thing? Greg! What if I don't call him back? Maybe he'll call the police.*

"Please don't shoot me." This voice sounds like an old-woman version of me. Like my grandmother's voice.

"All's we need is money. Just find us some money, and we'll let you go." *Does Slither, waiting out in his hot car, know this is happening?*

I have to think. I know we have nothing. Hell, half the time, we play a game called 'scrounge through the car and the couch to see if there is enough money for a happy meal or two.' The support check, supposed to come today, didn't arrive. I don't even have a job—how could I? Someone has to be home to help care for Josh and Caleb while Mom works. If Brian hadn't offered to take me to the carnival, I wouldn't have been doing anything tonight.

"We don't have any money. I . . . I can't think of anywhere we might have some." Then I remember my mom has a collection of coins. Steel pennies, wheat pennies, silver dimes, that sort of thing. I tell him this, and he scoffs.

"I don't want pennies."

"I don't know what to do." I'm trying to think so hard.

Then it comes to me.

"Wait! My dad! He lives just down the road. I could ask him for some money. As soon as he gets home from work, he'll give it to me. I know he will. Then, I'll give it to you."

He waves the gun at me, as if I might have forgotten the seriousness of the situation I'm in. "When does he get off work?"

"Uh, around five, so he'll be home about five-thirty."

"So, what are we supposed to do until then? We can't stay here." Again, he waves the gun, gesturing to the room.

My knees have had it with standing. They can't do it any longer. I slump into a chair.

He takes a deep breath. "I guess you'll have to come with us until we figure this out."

"But I thought you said you were out of gas?"

He shrugs. "Not really. No. Just wanted a little money, but you'll do, I guess."

I think I might throw up. *If I leave this house with this man and this gun, if I get into that car with that other man, I will never come home again.* I know this in my heart. Girls who get taken away—kidnapped at gunpoint—do not come back alive. Sometimes they're found. Sometimes they're just a segment on *Unsolved Mysteries*. But they *never* come back. I am now one of those girls. I am never going to finish my senior year of high school, never see my brothers or my mom again. Never get my photo in the Senior Who's Who with Greg. Instead, I'm just another chalk outline of possibilities unfulfilled.

"Let's go. We have to leave. Don't worry. We'll bring you home later. A pretty girl like you shouldn't be sitting at home alone on a Friday night. We're practically doing you a favor. Come on."

He grabs my wrist and pulls me up. My knees buckle. They are the only body part putting up any kind of resistance—

although the resistance is toddler-level stuff. Turning to boneless jelly and oozing onto the floor. Flat Top doesn't let that happen though. He's holding me tight. After he escorts me around the house, pointing out anything he may have touched so I can wipe it all down for him, we walk back into the living room and to the door. I can see through the picture window that at some point, Slither started up the car and pulled it into the driveway. He knows. *Of course he knew! He's the driver. How could he not know they weren't really out of gas?*

Flat Top shuts the door behind us. There are bugs in the hummingbird nectar. It's old, and I should have changed it. I think I remember reading about old nectar becoming poisonous. Now they will die, too. It's so strange how everything is connected. I'll call it The Hummingbird Effect. *So much for being a good, responsible girl*—all my inner black marks like bugs floating to the surface of my sweet façade.

"Wait!" I say. "Can I lock the door?"

He turns and looks at me. A snorting laugh coughs out of him. Spittle flies. "Sure," he says. "Whatever makes you feel better."

III.

On the porch, as I turn to lock the door, I remember a feeling. The day my brothers left for church camp, as I stood in this exact same spot waving goodbye, an uneasiness fell upon me. My breath hitched and I fought back both tears and the urge to run after the car, begging them to come back. A little voice whispered in my ear, *You'll never see them again.* I believed it, too. It felt real, but I suppressed it. How dumb, how silly. I would scare everyone to death and possibly ruin the boys' camping trip.

Looking back, I realize that I made a miscalculation. The one everybody makes when they get that 'bad feeling about something.' It's always that something bad is going to happen to someone else. But the something bad that was going to interfere with my ability to see Josh and Caleb again was happening to me.

We tromp across the lawn which always seemed so huge, but now, the driveway awaits just a couple feet from the house.

Flat Top opens the back door on the driver's side and tells me to scoot in. I do as he says; the gun is a great motivator. The car itself is a horror show. I wonder if I'll die in there. The space behind the back seat is filled with trash—plastic wrappers, empty bakery cookie trays, a plastic bag of clothes, empty fast-food cups and French fry containers. The front passenger seat is being held up with a two-by-four wedged between it and the back of the back seat. I sit down but then it's clear that Flat Top plans to sit beside me in the back so I slide over against the board, trapping myself between it and his sweaty body.

Once we're situated "nice and comfy" as Flat Top puts it, and my nose has acclimated to the stink of an old fryer, B.O., and dust, Flat Top sets the gun on the console. It's the first time I get a good look at it. It's actually quite small, but I know nothing about guns, so as far as I'm concerned, if it can shoot a bullet, it's just as dangerous to me as a bazooka. The handle part has a white, pearly inlay which could almost be called pretty in another world.

"I think maybe you should lay your head in my lap so no one sees you in this car, you know?" Flat Top says. "This is your neighborhood, after all. Do you want someone you know wondering what you're doing riding off with two strange men?"

Strange is an understatement, but I don't correct him. I've lost my sense of humor anyway. All I want to do in this moment is live, survive. And not because I have so many more things to do with my life or because I didn't get to say goodbye to anyone—sure, those are great reasons, but my brain isn't thinking like that—I want to live because I am a living creature with an evolutionary biology built to react in order to preserve the vital functions of the machine I am inhabiting. *Only this and nothing more* as Poe would say.

I don't speak, I simply do. The smell of him—his clothes, his crotch, his body—fills my head with more negativity. So instead, I focus on making the car an extension of myself, a metallic appendage, and hone in on my vehicular proprioception. We've pulled out of my driveway and turned toward town. Left for a long time and then a bridge or overpass changes the texture beneath the wheels before we turn right again. I think we're in town and headed west.

At some point—maybe only twenty minutes later, but maybe hours—we slow.

"Sit up. Lean your head against me so people think we're boyfriend and girlfriend." Flat Top lets me know he is speaking to me and not some other kidnapping victim by tapping me on the back of the head. I sit up and lean my head on his shoulder. Again, I say no words. "We have to stop for gas and some directions because, you know, we're not from around here. So, I need you to listen carefully. When we stop, if you scream or do anything to draw attention, I will kill you, but first I will kill anyone who comes to try to help you. You'll be responsible for their death, too—do you get it?"

Oh, I got it. I nod. Slither gets out as the attendant comes around to pump gas. I'm alone again with Flat Top. The dam breaks, and I begin to beg.

"Please don't hurt me, I don't want to die." I'm blubbering. I hate how weak I sound. But I am weak. I have no idea how to help myself.

You have drawn The High Priestess. Ask her to guide you.

"We won't hurt you as long as you do what we say. Do everything we tell you to do, and we'll get you back home when all this is over." Flat Top still doesn't look at me.

My mouth repeats my pleas of 'don't hurt me, I'm afraid to die' but my mind leaves for a moment and instead focuses on the image of The High Priestess, the old woman's gnarled fingers caressing her image. I send out a silent plea.

I need help. The old woman said the cards will guide me. I don't know if you can do anything to help or even if you're real, but I just don't know what to do.

The gas is pumped. Now the attendant and Slither have a map unfolded across the hatchback window. They're taking me somewhere. Slither gets back in the car.

"I had an idea. I remembered my uncle has a hunting cabin up this way somewhere. I figured we could go there to hang out for a bit." His voice is soft and it makes him seem kind. He seems like the nicer one. I should direct my pleas to him instead.

"Good thinking, Dave." Flat Top says. *Oh my god, he said his name. Dave.*

Dave smiles, starts the car, and turns on the radio. A local rock station—at least I don't have to listen to shitty music. I almost laugh.

"So, I was thinking, since we got all this time to kill, we might as well mess around a little bit," Flat Top says.

"I don't know what you mean." I know *exactly* what he means.

"You know, we mess around a little. That way when we do let you go, we know you won't tell anyone. You'd be too embarrassed. Plus, we'd just say you went along with it, make you look like a whore in front of your whole family. So, we mess around a little and that way we're sure you won't tell."

"I won't tell. You don't have to do that."

"Yeah, I think we do." Flat Top grins. "Might as well start now. It's not gonna hurt you. Take your bra off."

Some strange noise bubbles up from the back of my throat, but I don't say anything. I take my bra off. It's my open-in-the-front one, my super cute lacy one that I had no business wearing today in the first place. Greg is my boyfriend, not Brian. I hold it in my hands until Flat Top says to throw it on the floor. And just like that, it's gone. No longer mine but just another piece of trash in the car. I feel exposed even though my shirt is on, and shiver as if the bra was the only thing keeping me warm.

"You want to try something?" Flat Top asks.

I don't want to, but I say nothing. He slides the band of his shorts down and exposes his penis. It's really small. I've only ever seen one in real life—Greg's—so I don't have much to compare it to, but I'm sure it is abnormally small. He takes my hand and puts it on his dick. It's warm and hard. I don't want to touch it.

"Put your mouth on it, but don't you bite it or anything like that. No, you wouldn't want to do that, not with the gun so close. Got it?"

"I don't know how to do this," I say. "I've never done this before. I'm a virgin." This is a lie. I've had sex with Greg a few times. Nothing exotic or strange, but we've tried oral sex, too. Does that make me a bad person? Is lying about it wrong? It's the first lie I've told them. I feel the normal twinge of guilt for lying but I couldn't help it. My brain is in self-preservation mode. I'm not thinking, just reacting.

He pushes the back of my head down into his crotch. "Don't worry, we stopped at a rest stop on our way to your house and washed up a bit."

This was a needless bit of information. As soon as I'm close, I can smell the distinct difference between the fresh soapy smell around his dick and the yeasty stink of the rest of him. I tell myself not to gag. At least his penis is small, if it were any bigger, I'd vomit. I lick my lips but there is no moisture to be had anywhere. I hope he likes dry blow jobs.

He doesn't. He stops me. "You need a drink or anything? You're doing fine it's just . . . " He trails off. Slither, who has rarely spoken, offers me a take-out cup.

"Have a drink. I bet you're thirsty."

I suck a mouthful of warm, flat orange pop.

In my personal drink rankings, I'll always choose sweet tea or Coke first, followed by red pop, root beer—hell, I'd even pick ginger ale—which I equate with saltine crackers and sickness—before I would purposefully choose orange pop. And if said orange pop was flat, warm, and watered down, then I guess I'd just as soon give the world's driest blow job knowing full well his dirty cock was going to stick to every part of my mouth.

But the drink was already inside me, flavoring all my crevices with the syrupy, sticky orange flavor of Sunday school drinks given out in tiny Dixie cups as a reward for sitting still in an itchy dress while some old lady in polyester teaches us to be fishers of men.

Only these men aren't keepers and I've no taste for fishing.

I think, maybe this is God's little reminder that He has forsaken me for all my sins and nonbelief. Or maybe God's not real, just like tarot cards are just pieces of cardboard and the old lady was nothing more than a blind, elderly carny trying to make a buck or two.

You must let go of your rational side and seek answers from the spirits.

Flat Top wastes no time. I've had my drink; back to work. He pushes and I follow. The sooner I get this over with, the better. This time I don't touch it with my hand, I just put my lips around it and try not to smell or think too much. My eyes are shut tight.

"When I come," he says. "You don't spit. Just push it to the back of your throat and swallow."

I can't really nod or say yes, so my continuation is my silent consent to do whatever he says. Not that he needs my consent. That gun is a waiver to formalities like consensual agreements.

"Hey Oscar, she's good, man. Like really good. She ain't even using her hands!" He just called Dave Oscar. Why did he do that? But Flat Top doesn't make me wait until I've finished for an answer. Instead, he taps me on the head so I know he is talking to me. "Did you hear me call him Oscar? That's not his name, neither is Dave. I'm just calling him a bunch of different names to confuse you. So, you'll never know what his real name is.

You're so much smarter than these men. You will survive this if you remember that.

The voice is not mine, but it comes from inside me. It thrums like the loud, deep bass all the guys play in their cars. I let it roll through my body and I focus on the vibrato as Flat Top grunts and spurts into me, but it's not enough. My throat spasms and I gag. He feels my retches and shoves my head down harder against him. Tears drip from my face to his balls but I doubt he notices. I'm not crying, it's just what happens when your body forcefully tries to expel the chunk of flesh that's trying its damnedest to choke you to death.

The radio is blaring "Unbelievable" by EMF and I have to agree. This is all so unbelievable.

"There, see. That wasn't so bad. You didn't mind, did you?" Flat Top puts his arm around my shoulders and pulls me against him again. Slither sings along with EMF. I imagine he is trying not to think about what is going on behind him. He doesn't want to be here either. Maybe Flat Top is forcing him as well. *Poor guy.*

"She's real good, Marty. I can't wait for you to find out." He elbows me and winks. "See, you'll never know his name."

Dave-Oscar-Marty hits the gas and swerves onto a dirt road. Gravity seems to be on the side of the oppressors as it shoves me harder against Flat Top.

"So, you got a boyfriend?" he asks, as if now it's time to get to know each other, what with that pesky fellatio out of the way.

"Yes."

"And you guys haven't messed around? Not even once?"

"No." Suddenly the lie feels like the truth. I haven't done anything. I'm just a child. I'm pure snow-white innocence. I've done nothing to deserve this. I'm just trying to hold tight to my tower of blocks so these bullies can't come kick it to the ground.

"Well just chalk it up as a learning experience. Think of it this way, now you have a new skill."

The damn spiders. *It will be a real good learning experience for you, Josey.* I can't look at Flat Top. I'll break down, I'll lose it. I stare ahead and say nothing. It's become my most common defense.

"You know, I just thought of something." Flat Top hits the back of Slither's seat. He's speaking to me but he clearly wants Slither to pay attention. "We don't really need any money from your dad after all." He picks up the gun from the console and does that power wiggle with it. "'Cause we could steal some gas from the station. It's so easy. I just thought of that! That's pretty good." I get the elbow again. He's quite proud of his newfound criminal abilities.

Is this good for me or bad? They don't need me anymore—not alive, anyway.

He looks at me. "It's too late though, we can't take you back without making sure you're gonna keep your mouth shut. We're just gonna have to keep going. We don't *have* to kill you, not as long as you keep being a good girl. Can you be a good girl?"

I nod. I'm a good girl. At least I know how to behave like one.

"Say it to me. Look me in the eyes and say, *I can be a good girl.*"

"I can be a good girl." My chin quivers, and I swallow the impending tears.

"Don't do that; you gotta smile. Let me see you smile."
I smile.

"Look at it this way—we gotta do this stuff. If you went and told anyone—"

"I won't—" He puts his hand over my mouth and pats it.

"If you told, and we went to court over it, I'd just say that we stopped to use your phone. You were alone, and said you'd do anything to get out of the house for a while. You said that as long as we agreed to drop you off at home when we were done, you would do anything we wanted. See? Now you look like a whore in front of your whole family. Do you want them to think their good little baby is a whore?"

There is power here. Men call women whores because they fear them, because they fear the power they hold between their legs and secrets of creation within their cells. Take the moniker, if you must, but do not fear.

That voice again—ancient and thin, like the rustle of late autumn leaves in a breeze. The buzz inside me grows like a new life wanting to break free of its cocoon. But I am so afraid, so I try to muzzle it. That voice will get me killed, whoever it belongs to.

"Oh shit, though—Hey, Billy, you got any condoms on you?" Flat Top asks. I look up into the rearview mirror just as Slither does and for a second our eyes meet. I almost think I see remorse in his, but he just shakes his head no.

But if they can't rape me, what other way do they have of keeping me quiet? What, other than murder? Maybe this is what the voice meant. I look at the gun that sits solidly on the console. No turns, no swerves, no spins on the gravel and dirt roads have moved it. It has a sentience, an evil. It will not go from me.

"I'm due for my period in like four days. I'm past the point of being able to get pregnant, and I'm a virgin so I don't have any diseases."

Flat Top's eyes brighten at this. "Hey! Neither do we. We've only ever been with our wives, so we're all good. Great! Say, you know a lot about biology though, don't ya? Most girls your age are just out there giving it away, getting knocked up, having abortions. Hell, some girls your age are even taking it up the ass by now, so they can say they're virgins. You ever taken it up the ass?"

"Oh no. No. I told you. I've never done any of this kind of stuff."

"Then how do you know to calculate your period and stuff like that?"

"I'm going to be a doctor when I grow up. I'm in advanced biology, going to go to college for pre-med." I don't know why I'm telling him this stuff. He's not listening. As I'm talking, he sticks his hand up my shirt and cups my boob. His thumb keeps flicking my nipple and the goddamned thing gets all hard like I like it or something. I hate my body right now. I hate it.

"Your skin is so soft. You know, we got more time. Maybe we should try that blow job out again."

No. Absolutely not. I look out the window. "But there are so many houses and cars on this road. Someone might see us." He seemed so worried about anyone thinking he might be up to something; I thought that might work.

"Oh, yeah, yeah. That's good thinking, Doc. You are pretty smart! Just sit up. Don't do anything yet. We'll have a lot of time at the cabin."

A lot of time. What does that mean? The rest of my life? *Not if you fight smart,* my deep, husky-voiced inner companion offers. But can I fight at all? I'm so fucking scared.

IV.

The scenery has lost all semblance of familiarity. Somehow even the oaks, pines, and poplars all look foreign, menacing. I think of the Grimm Brothers fairy tales my grandma used to read to me. When the main character realizes that the woods they are in no longer look the same—when the trees take on a sentience and create a sense of danger for the protagonist, usually a child or young woman like me—it means you can soon expect to meet the villain.

I've certainly gone beyond the borders of safety, of a forest filled with bunnies and songbirds. Here is where you'll find the glowing eyes of lurking predators, the haunted calls of carnivorous birds, brittle twigs snapped by unseen things. Here, in these woods, we will come upon the witch's cottage where the real story begins. All that's happened up to this point was just preamble, setting the stage for what is to become of me.

Slither is driving much too fast for these gravel-covered roads.

"Oh god! Watch out!" I yell. A dog the size of a bear stands in the center of a split in the road. The beast is like a behemoth version of the prize I won a million years ago, back when I was strong enough to conquer my fears, back before I regressed to this childlike mouse pulled against a gunman in the back of a maroon mechanical prison in the middle of an evil enchanted forest.

Slither doesn't seem to see it, but the dog sees me. I know it does. It's crazy to think the dog can see through the car and into the back seat. It seems even further unlikely that we could make eye contact, but I swear we do.

Flat Top stabs me in the side with his elbow. "What're you screaming about?"

I look at him. How can he not see?

"The dog—" I point but there is no dog on the road anymore—it must have run off—" I . . . there was a dog. A big, big dog in the road. We almost hit it!"

The noise that comes from Flat Top is an awful honking, braying laugh that I've heard in every movie starring Bill Paxton that I've seen. That know-it-all, jock-asshole guffaw that is not truly a laugh but a warning—"Don't fuck with me and don't you ever, by god, I mean ever, question or disagree with me!"

"You're losing your mind, young lady! I thought you said you were smart? First of all, those are horses—" He points to a pasture on the side of the road where a couple of bored, swayback nags stand swishing flies away with their scraggly tails. "And secondly, they're behind a fence, not on the road. Hey, Mike—you hear this girl?"

Slither looks up in the rearview and meets my eyes. I think I see an apology in his. He turns up the radio currently playing "Sympathy for The Devil" by The Stones and swerves to the left, away from the horses and deeper into the woods.

Flat Top snakes his dirty hands up my shirt and squeezes my breast.

"Almost there—a few more minutes." As if I'm anxious to arrive. It occurs to me to wonder how he knows where to find Slither's friend's cabin. It also occurs to me to panic—I am nearing the end of my life. Even if I somehow survive, I will not return whole—this I know for certain.

V.

The cabin is pink. Completely Pepto-Bismol pink—what my brain has deemed abysmal pink. This place looks like a child's drawing. It is the pink-iced gingerbread home of Hansel and Gretel's witch—and me without my breadcrumbs.

A two-story abomination—no porch, no fancy shutters, just a monochrome nightmare as if someone stood on the roof and simply dumped cans of bubblegum-colored paint down the sides—stands surrounded on three sides by forest. The front yard is filled with overgrown weeds and split in half by a two-lane dirt drive set so far back from the road, no passersby could see it. We park parallel to the house so that the passenger side window faces it.

I don't want to die there—trapped within Barbie's Dream Coffin, legs spread wide and mouth filled with orange syrup and cum.

Flat Top grabs the gun from the console and stuffs it in the elastic waistband of his shorts.

"Come on. Let's go in." He holds his hand out to me and I take it. He escorts me around the front of the car. We stop. "See how I took you this way so you couldn't see the license plate? I've thought of everything."

I nod and think that if he is worried about me seeing the plate number, maybe they really are going to let me go. It's crazy if they do. I may not know their names, but I can describe them both well—in the case of Flat Top, right down to his micro-penis.

Slither has already gotten out and is coming back from behind the house. He unlocks the door.

Flat Top says, "Here, take her inside," and then takes the keys from him and heads back to where Slither just was. They've both been here before and know it well enough to know where the key is hidden. How much of this is a ruse, and why bother pretending? What do I know about anything? What do they want from me?

We walk in together and I'm alone with Slither for a moment.

He sits in a chair in the kitchen, the room just beyond the front door. The place is old—white porcelain sink, 1950s-style fridge, and a small stove. The table is like my grandma's—yellow Formica with an aluminum trim. I think about Grandma's old fridge. It had this weird short in it, so if you stood with the door open and touched the metal trim of her counters, a current of electricity would zip though you.

I imagine walking over to the refrigerator and offering to get Slither a beer. I'll keep the door open and hold it out to him. When he grabs it, I'll pass the jolt to him. But here in this place, the jolt is deadly. We'll both probably die, but I'll still be free. Instead, I stand paralyzed, unable to move. I am in the place of my death, yet I cannot help myself—I'm still just a child.

"Come here." He holds his arms out to me. He doesn't have the gun. I go to him.

"I'm so afraid," I tell him. His eyes seem kind. I don't want to touch him, though. He is greasy and dirty and what teeth he has left are decaying.

"We won't hurt you. You just have to do what we say. My friend, he . . . he can get a little crazy, so its real important that you do whatever he tells you to do." He pulls me down onto his lap and holds me against his chest. "I don't want you to get hurt. I don't want to have to hurt you. You just keep being sweet, okay?"

I nod against his chest, using exaggerated movements so he can feel me agree. I will be sweet. I'm a good girl. We sit like this for what seems like forever, long enough that I can start to identify the different smells attached to Slither— cigarettes, sweat, that thick, globular smell of a body that hasn't been washed for a long time, and blood. But that can't be right, can it? Blood? Maybe it's my fear or something. I've read enough horror books to know there is some scent to fear;

I've just been fortunate enough not to have ever smelled it. Must be fear, not blood.

"Hey!" Flat Top is back. "What's all this about? You two start the party without me?"

Slither eases up on the pressure holding me against him. "Nah, we were just getting to know each other is all."

"Oh yeah? What did you learn?" He pulls me off Slither's lap. "Huh? What did you learn about my buddy, here? What did he tell you about this place?"

Slither stands up. "Nothing. I didn't tell her anything, so how about shutting up?"

They stare each other down for a minute. Finally, Flat Top laughs.

"Good deal. Let's give her a tour, then."

Downstairs, there is the kitchen, of course. To the left of it is a small living room with a wood-burning stove, a dirty tan carpet with enough wrinkles to trip up a ballerina, two dowdy brown couches featuring country scenes on their velvet-like upholstery, and a badly abused coffee table. The wood-paneled walls have been generously decorated with various stuffed and mounted dead creatures.

To the right of the kitchen, which has not been 'decorated' in the classic Western Pennsylvania décor, is a set of stairs against the wall. Beyond them, to the side of the fridge, is a door—amateurly painted to look as if it is just part of the paneling and not a door at all. The black 'grooves' look like they were drawn with a marker, by a kindergartner. They don't show me what's beyond that door—in fact, they don't even point it out.

Upstairs, there are two big bedrooms with multiple beds. The first one has two twins and a bunk bed, and a white-painted brick fireplace with a large buck head mounted above it. The only deer that I've seen—it's an impressive rack, even with the giant cobweb that connects it's nine points. Given that all the other mounted pieces are small game and birds, I'm guessing the buck was a stroke of luck and had little to do with skill, or maybe I just need to believe that right now. The mantle is just a piece of unfinished wood with a small, white, coiled clay bowl—the kind you make in art class in sixth grade.

Flat Top takes me to the far wall beyond the beds and the railing that overlooks the stairs. Here, in the back corner is a small alcove formed by the last bit of railing perpendicular to the rest and the back corner of the room. In the center of this sits a ten-gallon plastic bucket with a potty chair seat sitting haphazardly on top of it. A roll of toilet paper has been kindly left beside it on the floor. I have to pee but I don't really want to go on this thing. I consider trying to hold it, but then Slither looks through the doorway into the next room and says, "Hey, there are bigger beds in here. We could go in here."

I can't do this with a full bladder.

"I have to pee."

"Well, go then, dummy. I just showed you the toilet."
Flat Top stands there, staring, as if he's waiting for me to drop
my jeans right there in front of him.

"I can't do it with you watching me."

"Well, that's too bad then, cause we ain't leaving you
alone."

"Let her go in the black room," Slither says. "You can
stand outside a door, and I can stand outside the other one."

"She can't go in there!" Flat Top shouts back. "Are you
nuts?"

"Think about it . . . It's the black room for a reason, isn't
it? What's she gonna see? Just let her go."

Flat Top takes a deep breath and sighs. "Okay, fine. But
you should have said something when we were down there,
dummy." He snatches the roll of toilet paper off the floor and
shoves it at me. "Let's go, then."

At the bottom of the stairs we make a U-turn and I
follow him to the door beside the fridge, the one he neglected
to show me on my two-room tour of the first floor.

Slither goes out the front door as Flat Top opens a portal
to utter darkness.

"Go," he says, grabbing my arm and steering me across
the threshold. It's so dark. I shuffle forward a few steps and
stop. As I turn to ask where the light switch is, I get the door
slammed in my face.

Once, I went on a cave tour with Ang and her family. When we got to the center of the caverns, what they called the grand ballroom, the guide turned off all artificial lights.

Immediately, the darkness swarmed in like wet mud, wrapping itself around me, smothering me. I knew I was in a large open space, yet claustrophobia squeezed my heart. Had I not been with Ang, who grabbed my hand, I would have screamed.

I feel that same terror now, but Ang isn't here. There's no one here to hold my hand.

The darkness nuzzles up to my neck and whispers in my ear, "No one can help you now. Only you can save yourself."

"It's too dark. I can't see anything. Where is the toilet?" I ask, empowered somewhat by the hushed wisdom of the abyss.

"Just go on the floor; we do it all the time."

I've been reduced to a caged animal—my humanity stripped away bit by bit. I venture no further but pull down my pants and squat as I was taught to do camping in the woods when I was young.

"What do I do with the toilet paper?" I call out.

"Just throw it on the floor."

I imagine a room filled with balled up, used toilet tissue, but my senses tell me that is not the case. This room doesn't smell like piss and shit; it smells like the muskiness of fear, of years of secrets and taboo acts committed in the safety of the dark. A musty and ancient evil is sleeping beneath the floorboards, just waiting to be awakened with the bodily fluids of the next victim. Blood, of course, is ideal, but this malevolence has been here for a long time and it will take anything in offering.

I've scared myself so much that the arms of my captors seem safer than what I feel awakening within the bowels of the black room.

I pound on the door. "I'm done. Please, let me out." Flat Top opens it, and I nearly fall into him.

"Ooh, anxious to get the party started, are we?"

I am not.

"You didn't like it much in there?"

I shake my head.

"You'll get used to it," he says, just as Slither reenters the room.

I don't want to get used to it. Plus, how does he know?

"Can I wash my hands?" I ask.

Slither walks over to the sink and turns it on. Nothing happens. "No water. Don't worry about it. Come on."

No water? I do worry about it. We can't stay here long without water. So are they gonna kill me here? Would they actually take me home? Either way, there won't be much time to 'get used to' the black room.

I follow Flat Top upstairs, monkey in the middle, with Slither behind me. I wonder what he would do if I turned and shoved him down the stairs and then ran. Could I get away? I look up at Flat Top and see the bulge of the gun at his hip. I could get away from them, I'm certain of it, but the gun—I can't outrun a bullet.

I keep climbing but stop outside the door to The Room. It's as if a force field is keeping me from entering. The deer head stares nonchalantly above us as if it has no interest in this human drama, but I can feel an anthropomorphic alertness from it, bearing silent witness to all that is happening to me. Its eyes are recording all to deliver to Mother Karma later. The deer has been their victim, too, so he is on my side.

"I'm just so nervous about everything," I tell them.

"Don't worry." Slither puts his hands on my shoulders from behind. They are clammy against the skin of my neck. "We are, too."

"Well, it makes it even harder when I know there's a gun with you. It's so scary. I won't be able to relax." I can't believe what I'm seeing, but Flat Top takes the gun out of his pants and lays it on a trunk that serves as the closest bed's nightstand.

"I'll be able to see it from the other room, I think." I'm really pushing it, and what for? Am I going to make a run for it out the second story window? Am I somehow going to overpower both men and get to it before them? And what if I do? Could I actually shoot somebody? *Two* somebodies?

Yet even so, Flat Top takes the gun and puts it on the floor beneath the braided throw rug. My mouth must have dropped open at the shock. Flat Top laughs. "It's not like we'd kill you in here. Our prints are everywhere, right?" He touches the ceiling with his fingertips. "Don't make us do something rash, okay?"

Slither chimes in, "Yeah, we're just here to have a good time. Some harmless fun. That's all. No one's getting killed." He smiles his jack-o'-lantern smile and I shiver.

VI.

The room where my life is about to irrevocably change is lit by a single window covered with peeling, vinyl butterfly clings. Two double beds are set against the wall with the window between. Beneath it is a single drawer nightstand, covered in dust, marred only by a book titled *Prayers for Daily Meditation*. In the cubby beneath the drawer there is a hat similar to Slither's, only red instead of blue.

We three stand in the space between the two beds in silence.

"Well, I guess maybe you should take your clothes off," Flat Top instructs me. It's like they planned everything up to this point, and now they have no idea how to proceed. Why are they so nervous? It's not like I'm pushing them into this.

"We don't have to do this," I say, trying to play on their confusion and uncertainty. "I swear I won't say a word. If you take me home now, no one ever has to know."

"Nah, this will be good for all of us. We're not gonna hurt you or beat you up or anything," Flat Top assures me.

Yes. Thank goodness—I was mostly worried about bruising.

"Go ahead and get undressed."

I do as I'm told until I get to my underwear. "Can I keep these on for a bit? It makes me feel less nervous." I do my best to sound innocent and scared. It's not hard.

Flat Top haws his usual donkey laugh. Slither smirks.

Slither speaks up, apparently trying to connect with me on some level. "I've never really done this with another man in the room before."

They have not undressed. They tell me to lay back on the bed. It's stifling upstairs, but I can't stop shivering. I close my eyes. They are touching me; hands, so many hands, slide over my body. My breasts, my thighs, my stomach. I hear the breaths leaving their noses faster and deeper. Words swirl around me.

"Oh god, you're so pretty."

"Your skin is so soft."

Palms leave clammy snail trails across my face, lips, neck, and I want to scream.

"You'll never have problems getting men if you stay this way."

"We're just taking our time trying to decide what all we can do. I know there are a lot of things you could do, especially after what you did to me when we were in the car."

I open my eyes only when the touches stop. I imagine my dead corpse under a black light—does a black light pick up remnants of any kind of body fluid? My body would look like those cave walls that are covered in palm prints. A Cro-Magnon crime scene. Lay me to rest in a museum. Show society how primitive men still are, how little we have evolved.

"Yeah. Why don't you show Max here how good you do at that thing?"

They take off their clothes and I lie inanimate, waiting like a doll to be picked up and used again.

From this angle, I can see a big spider working away in the window. I wonder if she is the same spider that left my deer friend with his web crown. I think of the little girl's *Charlotte's Web* shirt and hope this spider will write a message for me. Something like, "Help is on the way!"

Slither is leaning against the headboard, sitting with his legs spread and his penis hard. It's longer but thinner than Flat Top's.

"Get up on your hands and knees," Flat Top says. Clearly, he is running this operation. I do as he instructs, happy to still have my underwear. Only, I wish I'd worn a pair of my white cotton ones with the purple roses. Something childish instead of these blue silk bikinis.

Once I'm on all fours, Flat Top comes back around and, to my shock, grabs Slither's penis in one hand and the back of my head in his other. Slither braces. I don't think he expected this, either. He doesn't lose his hard-on, though. Without any other options, I take it into my mouth.

Something about this moment, this one in particular, breaks me. Maybe it's being on all fours like a dog, maybe it's having the second dick in my mouth in one day, but my face gets hot, my throat tries to choke me, and tears start to stream.

Flat Top is right there watching us like a porn director. He smacks me lightly on the back of my head.

"Don't cry. Don't you cry. You smile. It's not that bad, and you did so good in the car. You liked it then. Just do it like that." To Slither, he says, "She's good, huh? Doesn't use her hands. It's crazy."

Am I supposed to use my hands? How? I'm not some professional. I don't know what I'm doing. I don't want to have to touch them any more than the gun under the rug in the next room dictates.

The blow job goes on forever. I try to think about the spider in the window. She must be done by now. Does she think those faded butterfly clings are real? Is that what made her abandon the deer? Has she caught anything? Is there a message from Charlotte yet?

Some Pig!

I sure feel like some pig right now. When is this ever going to end?

Just like that, it does. Slither pushes my forehead away. "That's good. You don't have to keep going. Thank you, though." He didn't ejaculate; why is he thanking me? What if I was supposed to use my hands and now they realize I'm not good and not worth keeping around? What if, while I'm busy being *Some Pig* with one of them, the other decides it's time for some bacon and gets the gun?

No crying, only smiles. No crying, only smiles.

Flat Top is naked. I don't know when that happened. Slither gets up. I'm still sitting on the bed, butt on heels. Flat Top sits down where Slither was.

"I'd like another one of those specials of yours from the car, but do you think we should kiss first?"

The horror and disgust must show clearly on my face. "Hmm. No? Leave that as something special for your boyfriend?"

A sob leaps from my chest. *Greg. I'm so sorry, Greg. I'm sorry I'm not a good girl. I don't deserve you.*

"Ah, ah, ah. I said no crying. Now show me a big smile, and we'll agree—no kisses."

I smile. In school, for the Presidential Fitness Test, I always fail on the chin-ups, but this smile, this single coordination of ten tiny muscles, is by far the hardest task I've ever attempted.

He pushes my head down onto him again. As I try to ignore the ache in my jaw, he tells me to look up at him. "Look me in the eyes while you do that and smile."

I do my best. It's hard to smile and maintain eye contact while bobbing your head over a lump of warm, musky, raw meat.

Slither is behind me pulling my panties down. His finger slips inside me and I scrunch my eyes closed. A familiar head tap follows. "Hey, what did I tell ya? Look up at me."

I feel so small.

"You know," Flat Top says conversationally, as if I'm not looking at him with his dick in my mouth. "I could be really mean about this. I could make it last a long time. All I gotta do is think about what I had for dinner last night or a baseball game and not even think about what you're doing at all. That would make it take forever. But I'm not going to be mean. Not as long as you follow the rules."

Slither's finger is making me burn down there. It hurts. I can feel that I'm dry. I'm being attacked from every angle, and there won't be a bruise to show for it—just like they promised.

As if he hears my thoughts, Slither takes his finger out of me. I have little time to be thankful though because there is a slippery, slimy feeling coating me—soft and wet.

I am already dead. His lips and his tongue turn into maggots crawling into my invisible wounds and eating away all that I was, all that I am, and everything I could have been.

Flat Top cums, and I swallow for the second time today.

Slither is the first one to officially commit rape, if the definition is penile penetration of the vagina. So, while he is going to town on me, I still have to look at Flat Top and smile while he talks to me. The things he says make it really hard not to cry.

"See, it's not so bad. You like it, right?" He wants me to confirm that yes, of course, it's all so romantic and wonderful—every girl's dream.

"Chalk it all up to a learning experience. Ya know? Your boyfriend will be so happy that you learned all this new stuff, so, it really is a good thing. We're all just having a good time." As if Flat Top's adamance about how good this is for all of us has excited Slither, he finally thrusts hard into me and grunts. I feel a warm trickle as he pulls himself out and falls down on the bed beside me.

The butterfly clings on the window are flightless, trapped just like me. These men have torn through my silk cocoon; they've invaded and interrupted my process of becoming. I will never be beautiful. My wings are useless, smudged from having been touched too much.

It's over, I think.

I check Charlotte's progress on her web. It's done, just as I suspected. I do see a message! I think it says, "What web will you weave?" but then Flat Top tells me to roll over, and I realize that nothing is over. It will never be over.

Slither wastes no time. As soon as I'm on my back, he starts kneading my breast, squeezing and rolling my nipple. I feel like one of those stress balls, only I'm the one who needs it, not him. Flat Top hoists his heavy, sweaty body on top of mine and tries to work his soft, mushy dick into me. It's an exercise in futility. Instead, he folds it up against himself and starts grinding it around my parts. The only moisture is what Slither left behind and that's getting sticky.

"I can make you cum, you know? Then it's good for you, too. And then it's not rape, is it? It's not rape if you cum, 'cause it means you liked it. You wanted it."

I'm not going to have an orgasm. I don't want any of this. I'm scared—terrified, in fact—of what will happen when they're done. But I don't want this to keep going. I don't want them doing anything for me. Yeah, I'm panicked, but I'm angry, too. I'm so mad that they would think I could possibly get off on this. The only thing that would get me off is if this big lump of flesh had a cardiac arrest while grinding his little chub all over me.

"Hey, show her that thing, that trick that makes you cum real hard," Slither says, and I want to say 'no thank you, I'm good,' but I can't. Flat top's body is pressing all the air out of me.

And then, as if that was the plan all along, Flat Top reaches down and wraps his hands around my neck and squeezes. This seems to excite Slither because his hand is mirroring the squeeze on my breast, and it hurts, and I can't breathe, and he's choking me, and I'm trying to fight, but I'm dying. I'm dying, and they are still raping me. Still trying to get their dick hard enough to stick it back in.

I could die with a goddamned dick inside me.

The world starts to fade away. All I can see is the darkness behind the gap in Flat Top's teeth, all I can feel is the ache in my neck and chest and breast. Suddenly, I'm in the black room again, and then I am the darkness.

DAY TWO

SATURDAY, JUNE 27, 1992

VII.

Something is smothering me. I gasp for air against the obstruction that I am swaddled within. I manage to wriggle a hand free and tear though the gauzy web. Once through, I tumble to the ground. The jolt wakes me up and I cannot see.

I reach my hands out blindly, with trepidation. *Please don't let me be buried alive.* Claustrophobia takes over and I'm hyperventilating. It takes me several moments of flopping around like a fish before I realize I am not enclosed beneath the earth. But I am blind. I try to call out for help but my throat burns and my voice box refuses to cooperate. My body is no longer my own. Are my eyes just swollen white orbs now, like the old woman's?

I see them, suddenly, in the darkness—her glowing white eyes floating, flickering, becoming orange, becoming fire, and then they are torches and I can see again. I am in the black room. Once my sight returns, my other senses come back. I feel the gritty dirt on the floor, leaving tiny craters in my skin. The air is hot, stifling, and my naked body is oily with sweat. The room smells of must and piss and sex. The musk of sex might be coming off of me, but I just cannot accept that, so I attribute it to the room.

About a foot away from me, the floor is littered with the balled-up tissue I used to wipe myself with so many days ago. Between the torches that once were eyes, there is a stand with a wash basin on it. There is soapy water in the bowl and a sponge lying neatly atop a folded red towel beside it.

I wash my face, my hair, my body as best I can, happy to be cleansed of the remnants of my real-life nightmare.

There is a mirror between the torches that wasn't there before.

The woman in the reflection is not me.

The old woman stares blankly through her milky eyes. The gray hair I remember is now a halo of inky abyss surrounding her.

"Will you accept the help I offer?" she asks.

Without thinking, I answer that I will.

"Then take this gift that I bestow upon you."

The mirror, it seems, is not a mirror at all but an open portal. She holds out a deck of tarot cards toward me. Our hands touch during the exchange, and a whoosh of air dizzies me. When the sensation dissipates, I am on the other side of the portal. Looking into the torch-lit black room, I see a twin bed against the far wall. An older man sits on it beside a young boy. The man's hand rests on the boy's knee, and I search the boy's face for signs of consent. But the blue ball cap without an emblem is pulled down, and his head hangs in such a way that I see nothing but shadow.

In the corner stands another young boy. This one, short and chubby—what clothes-makers refer to as husky. His striped shirt isn't quite long enough to meet the elastic band of his red jogging shorts.

I don't want to look at the boys. I don't want to have pity for them. Instead, I focus on the familiar nightstand by the bed, where the lamp, prayer book, and red cap sit just as they had in my own torture room.

I know that none of this is really happening. It *must* be a dream. I turn away and see my own sleep-appointed room. There are torches here as well, lighting a table that occupies most of the space. My dog is back. He is not the small thing plucked from the carnival prize shelf, but the dog from the crossroads, the one Slither almost killed. He rests on a large, overstuffed papasan chair in the darkest corner of the room. If it weren't for the intense glow of his yellow eyes, I might not know he was there.

I carry my deck to the table and take a seat in a director's-style chair. As I spread the cards across the table, the old woman speaks and her voice reverberates from within me.

"You choose the cards from this point on."

I turn over the first card—The High Priestess, of course. The old woman's ancient, all-knowing voice surrounds me. I feel those eyes—white hot embers glowing like hellfire in her skull—searing her words upon my soul.

"The High Priestess sees beyond the veil, centered in the space between logic and emotion, earth and moon, the seen and the unseen. She reminds you of your own intuition and abilities to see beyond the surface."

I understand this is where I now reside—in the space between. I am driven only by my intuition. I must remain alert and focused.

There is a knock on the door but it opens before I can answer. The bright light streaming in from the kitchen burns my eyes and they immediately produce the river of tears they'd dammed up during the rape.

Slither has a bottle of water. He must have gone to a store or something while I was out.

"Here, you need a drink?"

I nod because suddenly the pain in my throat coupled with the intensity of my fear has sewn my tongue to the roof of my mouth and only water can dissolve the stitches.

"You can come sit at the table if you want."

I do kinda want. My legs and knees hurt from being on the floor for who knows how long. I say nothing but step out fully into the light. The cacophony of an engine amplified by a rusted exhaust, rubber on loose gravel, and the thumping bass of Megadeath's "Symphony of Destruction" divert Slither's attention from my naked body.

We watch Flat Top park, sliding in the gravel to end up diagonal to the house. He is wearing the same clothes as yesterday. Poor planning on their part. How long had they originally planned to keep me here?

Slither heads out to help carry groceries in. I am unsure what to do. Should I stay at the table or scuttle back to my black hole in the wall? I watch out the window as Slither approaches the car. Flat Top is bent over, leaning into the back seat.

Together they carry in groceries and a couple plastic, department-store-style bags.

I guess they're just winging it. But the number of supplies coming into the cabin frightens me. I retreat to my cards, leaving my subconscious to count the sacks of groceries and wonder what else could be within the bags. *Duct tape? Rope? Rat poison?*

Flat Top barges in through the door. I stand indecisive and naked in front of him. The fear is gone, it's more like being in mourning.

"Hungry?" He grabs a generic 'toaster pastry'—cold, and still in its package, out of a grocery bag and tosses it on the table. I refuse to touch it.

"No," I answer, my voice emotionless and just as frigid as the rejected breakfast.

"What's up your ass this morning?" His loud nasally breathing intensifies as he stands there wondering how he has lost the upper hand. He doesn't like it, and he wants to teach me a lesson. My intuition is on point, I *know* this. I am not guessing.

Finally, he huffs, "Well, starve then. I'm gonna make myself some eggs and bacon."

As he angrily grabs pots and pans out of cupboards, I realize I shouldn't have made him so mad while there is still a gun in this house.

Panic nips at my spine, so I step back, retreating into the safety of the room. Black Dog raises his head and chuffs, disappointed with my lack of faith. I sit back down at the table provided by my loosening mind and flip a card, but I don't need to look at it. I already know what it is.

The Eight of Swords.

The card of fear and imprisonment. Consumed by dread.

I can even see the picture in my mind. The girl trapped in a cage made of swords. There is an escape, but she is too filled with terror to see it.

The only way out is through, the blind woman speaks. She sees what I cannot. There is an escape, I just can't find the way.

VIII.

I cross my arms on the tabletop and drop my head onto them.
Black Dog comes over to me, his nails clicking on the wood
floor. His hot breath warms my cheek as he lays his chin on
the table, mimicking me. I lift my head to look at him, and
scratch him between the ears. He's a good dog, and he makes
me feel safe when he is with me.

Suddenly he perks up, his ears at full attention. Black
Dog growls—a low guttural and angry disapproval from
deep in his core. My heartbeat reverberates in my chest—the
human version of a growl, I guess. The hairs on my body rise
to attention, as do his.

"What do you hear, boy?" I ask. I was under the
impression that I was safe here in this illusion, but I'm starting
to think that was a foolish, naive assumption.

Black Dog trots over to the mirror—our window
between worlds—and watches intently, his tail stiff and
unmoving. Part of me doesn't want to look, doesn't want to

see, but I have to. What has my familiar so interested is the other black room, which again is inhabited by ghosts of the past. The bed and nightstand are there, but only one body. He is nude, his knees pulled up and arms wrapped around them, chin resting on bony joints. He's young—early teens, maybe fifteen at the oldest. The prayer book is open in front of him on the bed. He is holding it open with his big toes. I can only see him in profile, but it's all I need to positively identify him as Slither.

Subconsciously, I have always thought of him as 'The Nice One.' I realize the stupidity and childishness of the thought. He kidnapped and raped me right along with Flat Top, but he is quiet, and he doesn't say much. I'm always giving him an imagined inner monologue where he is ashamed of his behavior—guilt-ridden, even. Although I hated it, he even tried to do oral on me, which I figured was his way of making it okay. It's crazy, but if either one could earn my pity, make me hesitate to turn them in, it would be Slither.

Black Dog's quiet, airy bark brings my attention back to the vision just as the door opens and young Slither looks up. The older man from before walks in wearing camo fatigues, an orange vest, and carrying a rifle—bolt open and barrel pointed up.

"Have you learned your lesson?" the man asks.

"Yes. Sorry, Uncle Rick."

"Did you read your prayers and meditate on their meanings? Do you understand what God wants you to know, what he has asked me to show you?"

"Yes, sir."

"Would you like to go hunting now and do your repentance later, then?"

"Yes, please."

"All right, then. You may get dressed. I'll wait for you outside. Paul is in the blind with me; it's his turn to have first shot. He's earned it. You can use the tree stand."

"Thank you, sir."

"Just chalk it up as another learning experience," Uncle Rick says, and chills run up my spine like Flat Top's fingers.

The scene in the window changes. Uncle Rick and Slither are walking through the woods. They stop and Slither climbs the ladder to the tree stand. Uncle Rick watches until he gets situated, loaded gun at the ready.

"Now, remember, Paul gets first shot."

Slither nods, but I doubt Rick can see it. The Uncle seems quite confident in his own authority. He walks away without a look back as Slither points the gun at the back of Rick's head, following his movement. I hold my breath and realize Slither is holding his, too, because I can see Rick's coming out in hot steamy puffs, but nothing like that escapes from Slither.

Rick stops and cocks his head. I wonder if he can feel the gun pointed at him. He turns, slowly, in the direction opposite to Slither and then quickly up at the boy, who just as quickly swings the gun away and fires it.

Miraculously, Slither has shot and downed a buck—the one stuffed and hung above the mantle upstairs. I was so intent on watching the drama between the boy and his uncle, I did not see the deer. Black Dog's tail wags, and I wonder if that's what he'd been growling about all along.

"Hey!" A chubby and pimply but unmistakable teenaged Flat Top trots out of a deer blind just beyond the window's vantage point. "It was my turn! I had him in my sights!"

Slither is already crawling down from the tree stand, his face unsmiling. Uncle Rick's lips are pursed, and I fear for the young Slither—his 'learning experience' is going to be steep tonight.

When Slither reaches the ground, Uncle Rick grabs his shoulder. I can see that he is gripping the boy so hard, his knuckles are white—Slither can't stop the grimace of pain that flashes across his face.

"Be careful who you choose as your enemy because that's who you become most like," Rick says to Slither through clenched teeth. "Do you understand what Nietzsche meant by that?"

Slither nods. No more 'yes, sirs' or 'no, sirs.'

"Paul and I are going back to the cabin. You're responsible for dressing and dragging your own kill. Do a good job because that will be your dinner tonight."

I watch, close to tears, as Uncle Rick and Flat Top walk away. I hate myself for feeling bad, and I am glad Slither isn't here because I'd feel a need to hug him.

The view doesn't change. Black Dog and I watch Slither stand still, alone in the middle of the cold woods, contemplating his decisions. At the same time, the voices outside the door increase in volume, pulling me back into the reality of my situation.

"Where'd you go this morning?" Flat Top asks Slither.

"Went to that little gas station for a couple bottles of water and some cigs," Slither mumbles, clearly not interested in answering Flat Top's questions.

"You knew I was gonna make a supply run. Why didn't you just wake me up?" Flat Top sounds like an exasperated wife.

"Eh, didn't sleep too good anyways. Was having dreams about the black room."

Flat Top snorts. "That was a long time ago, man. Just drop it."

"Kinda hard to do here. This fucking place brings it all back, doesn't it? And then you go and put her in there. Why couldn't you have just left her upstairs?"

"Hey, man. Coming here was your idea, so that's on you. Besides, we're in charge now. This is our place and no one else's. We don't have to think about the past. Got that? We make the rules." Flat Top's voice is filled with pride, as if he won it in some fierce competition.

Slither isn't impressed; he sounds off, maybe a little paranoid. "Yeah? Who put that fucking deer head up? It's like *he* knew we were coming. Like he wanted to remind us that this is his place."

"Rick's dead, dude. Been dead. He didn't do it. I don't know *who* put it up. Maybe Chuck and his buddies? I mean, hell, it's a great rack—should have been mine, but even so. And, anyway, you ain't in the black room no more—you never have to go back in there. Never."

Something's happening here. A rift is widening. They have dug themselves a grave, and neither knows who's going in it.

"Yeah." Slither's checked out. He's done with the conversation.

Flat Top isn't dropping it. "Hell, man, we could walk right now, if you wanted. Just do it and leave her there. We got all them salt licks. We could block up the body with 'em, keep the smell down. Come back in November after they quit looking for her."

Slither hits or throws something; the thud makes me jump. "Shut up, would ya? I gotta figure this out."

"Marty, hey, we got this." Flat Top cajoles. "The girls won't be home for a few more days. Plenty of time. Come on, I don't want you all down and mopey. This was supposed to be fun. It was supposed to be about *us*."

"Yeah, well, what if I don't want to be here anymore? What If I don't want to be reminded of what a loser I am? A couple of fucking sinners *we* are—cheating on our wives and shit."

"Come on, man. You know it ain't like that."

"Oh? It ain't?" Slither asks. His rage is frightening. I can almost hear his spittle flying, sizzling when it hits the floor. I want to yell at Flat Top, to tell him to stop before Slither explodes. Instead, I hold my breath, head against the door to the kitchen, curled up in a fetal position. I don't even know when I moved, but I am fully in this moment now, waiting for the gun to appear in my life once more.

"What's it like then, Paul? You know if Uncle Rick was here, we'd both be in the black room on our knees."

Something else crashes. "Fuck that bastard! Don't even call him that! He ain't my fucking uncle. Plus, Rick ain't here. She is. And we gotta figure out what we're gonna do with her."

I hear Slither chugging a drink—beer, most likely—then slamming the bottle on the table.

"Ya know what I'm gonna do?" he spits. "I'm gonna fuck her. I'm gonna fuck her until all this shit is flushed out of my head. Then I'll figure out what to do with her!"

Furniture is shoved out of the way as Slither storms past the table. His footsteps approach and I scramble back away from the door. Flat Top yells, "Hell yeah!" and the door swings open.

Before my eyes can adjust to the light, one of them grabs my arm and hoists me onto my feet. The pins and needles jab at my soles so painfully that I can't fully stand on my own. Flat Top gets both hands beneath my arms and drags me like a dead body around and up the stairs; my Achilles tendons bounce on the lip of every step, sending shockwaves of pain up my back.

I don't want to be here for this. Once was enough. I curl my soul up into a ball inside my head and leave my body on autopilot. It can fend for itself. That whole fight or flight thing. If I have to endure another episode like yesterday, I'll go mad.

So I choose instead to return to the wooden table in the safe black room I have created where a deck of cards awaits me. Black Dog sits in front of a card flipped face up as if he chose it for me.

The Five of Wands.

I stare at it. Two men in the picture fight each other, each holding two of the five wands like staffs.

"What does this mean?" I ask Black Dog, not expecting him to answer.

But he does. His yellow eyes turn white, like over-easy eggs. His mouth doesn't move, and yet the old crone's voice comes from within his muzzle.

The card of confusion and struggles. Competition leads to disorganization. The men of this card have been caught off guard. They have awoken to something which they did not plan. In the flow of agitation and negative energy, do not let yourself get struck down. What we fight, we become . . .

I'm trying to understand, trying to focus on the message she sends through Black Dog, but I feel like I am inside a boxcar and someone is doing their best to break in. The room is shifting and rocking, my body struggles to stay upright, and I can hear myself grunting against the intrusion.

Black Dog barks once and disappears. Cracks run along the walls and ceilings of my safe room. Tarot cards scatter to the floor. I see the Devil's face staring up at me from the fifteenth card in the major arcana. And I know I must return; I must face what is being done to my body—my only true sanctuary. But with each step I take, pain returns. My throat flinches with each breath, my vagina cries scalding tears of blood down my legs, and the closer I stumble to the awareness, to the connection between my soul and my body, the sickness in my gut surges with each thrust against my bones. A tearing sensation runs between my buttocks and I know I am being raped anew. That sickness I feel with each thrust is a visceral response to a foreign invasion. Nothing of me has been left untouched, unsullied, unspoiled.

I can't face the reality of what is happening to me. I retreat again to the darkness, where I am allowed to cover my eyes and cry. Then the sky begins to fall; the cracks in the ceiling break and pieces hit my hand, my hair, my back. It's a solid patter raining upon and around me. I peek out at my safe place but their intrusion is now complete. The black room is filling with larvae, rice-sized wriggling maggots and plump pearlescent grubs. They're flooding in, covering everything. As the room shifts and pitches, it gives birth to a million seeds of hate and disgust.

I can't, I just can't.

I stand and I scream. My fists are clenched tight, my eyes refusing to look at the horror around me.

"Stop it! Get off! Get off! Don't touch me!"

I'm hitting Slither's head as he laps at my bloody crotch. Gobbling both me and Flat Top's cock like a pig at a trough. He looks up at me, my blood smeared across his lips.

"Oh god, why? Why would you do that?" I can't hide my revulsion.

I lunge away from both and kick out, managing a solid connection, skimming Slither's forehead to hit Flat Top's balls. Slither—the one-time *nice one*—jumps back from the reach of my feet, his dick soft but his eyes hard.

"What the fuck? Fucking bitch! You trying to call me a faggot?"

I shrink against the headboard, pulling my feet against me, turning into an impenetrable ball. I don't understand the question. Where did that come from? I choose not to respond.

"You must think I'm gay, I mean if you aren't participating, then what? Me and Paul are just doing this with each other for fun? No! We're having a threesome and these are all the different ways it's done. It's what straight people do!" He leans close to my face. I shut my eyes, but he grabs my jaw and squeezes until I open them again. I can smell the beer on his breath and on the rage-spit that is rolling down my face.

"This is what straight people *do*." He grabs the prayer book from the nightstand—the one that used to reside beside the bed in the black room.

"You see this?" He hits me in the face with it, hard on the nose, it tingles painfully, bringing more tears to my eyes and threatens a sneeze that I know would hurt like hell. "You know what this means? It's in *my* cabin! That means I live by it! Fuck you for thinking anything else about me. You don't fucking know me. Think you're so fucking smart. Think you can treat me this way cause you're cute? It's fucking bitches like you—"

"I'm sorry, I got scared. It hurt." I'm blubbering, but he's going nuts. This is what the old woman was talking about. I need to try to stay calm. Flat Top is somewhere behind him. Near the door, maybe. I hear his voice from over there.

"You want me to take her out? We don't need her judgement." He has the gun. *Oh shit, he has the gun.*

"Gimme that." Slither snatches it off him and turns around. He shoves it in my face. It's touching my chin. "Open your mouth."

I shut my eyes instead. He slaps me hard across the face. "Open your goddamn mouth, you little whore." I do. He forces the gun in until his knuckles hit my teeth.

"See. That's natural. That's how it goes. You're a woman. This is what you are good for. Now suck it."

I'm afraid to move a single muscle of my mouth. His finger is on the trigger and my teeth are right against his finger.

"That is so fucking hot," Flat Top says. This pisses Slither off for some reason, and he rips the gun out of me, chipping my front tooth and splitting my upper lip. He points the gun at Flat Top.

"Hey, hey, It's cool. It's okay," Flat Top assures him.

But Slither isn't having it. "No. It's *not* okay, Paul! I mean what the hell are we doing here? This ain't my cabin. This is Uncle Rick's place. Uncle Rick the fucking pastor. He taught us about this."

Flat Top takes a couple steps toward Slither, his arms up in the universal 'I surrender' pose.

"Uncle Rick did the same shit to us, man. Practically our whole lives. So what's the problem? I thought this was the plan? So what if she don't like it—fuck her."

They both look back at me. Slither is flipping the gun all over as if it's just a laser pointer. "Oh, yeah. Fuck her! That's what got us into this in the first place. Only, now what? Now *what,* Paul?"

"What?" Flat Top asked, clearly not following the 'What do we do now?' Outside this moment, it might be funny, like an Abbott and Costello routine.

He takes a moment to run the question through his head again, takes a big breath, and sighs. Then he shrugs. "We kill her. That was the plan."

My mouth is instantly dry; I can't swallow, I can't unstick my tongue to protest or beg.

"Shit, shit, shit. I didn't think this through. We can't kill her. Not here. It's Rick's cabin, Paul. *God's* cabin. Uncle Rick brought us here to teach us about sin, man. Now look at us."

He's losing it. Cracking. I have to be on guard. This is what the old woman warned me about. But how? How can I protect myself when it's two against one? I slide to the edge of the bed cautiously, each millimeter of distance achingly slow.

Flat Top, in his infinite ignorance of Slither's mental state, says, "Man, Rick was a fucking pedo-fag. It ain't ever been about *God.* It was about what he could get away with. And, up until she ruined it—" he jabs his finger at me. Slither follows with his eyes. He looks at me for a long time, and I wonder if he notices my gradual progress across the mattress. "Things were going great. You were the one who said it wouldn't be right without a girl. It was your idea to bring cheating on our wives into this. We could have had a much better time without her—just us, man."

They both look at me again. I freeze but hold their eye contact. I need them to see me as a human being—living and breathing. I try a smile but it doesn't feel authentic, so I let it go.

Flat Top continues, "So, I find you a girl, but you knew what we'd have to do all along. Look at her. She knows it, too."

"Please." It's all I can say before my throat closes up.

Flat Top, however, doesn't know when to quit. "This ain't Rick's cabin anymore. It's yours, *ours*. We ain't ever gonna bring the girls here or anyone else but us now. No more Chuck. Nobody but us. We can do whatever we want. We just needed to know we could do it—without Rick, without our wives, or anyone else even knowing what we do. It ain't wrong, Marty."

Slither drops the gun to his side. He's actually listening to this crazy asshole. I'm going to die soon if I don't think of something.

Flat Top steps forward again. There is now only about three feet between them and two more feet from Slither to me. He holds his hand out. "Give me the gun. Let me do her, and we'll have a couple days yet to figure out what to do. We can toss her down the well, store her in the black room, whatever."

Flat Top grins. He looks right at me and, in that awful, horrible space between his teeth, I can see the Devil card. In my periphery, I see Slither raise his gun arm to give it to him. If I don't do something right now, in this very second, I'm dead.

I jump up with the intent to surprise Slither and hit him as he loosens his grip on the gun to hand it to Flat Top. I just have to be faster than either of them, and I'll have to somehow find the courage to shoot.

But I don't get that chance because Slither doesn't hand the gun over to Flat Top. Instead, he shoots him in the face.

IX.

I'm close enough to feel a spray of Flat Top's blood hit my brows and lips. I am close enough to have seen the entire thing in slow motion, a close-up of his face exploding. Bone and hair flying into the air like migrating birds. Even battered and bloodied, the winged things still flee. I'm frozen in place. Slither seems to have forgotten I'm in the room. He leans over and looks at Flat Top's spoiled face.

"You have to learn about sin first. You need to understand what is right and what is wrong in the eyes of God!"

My knees threaten to drop me, so I fall back on the bed. I can't seem to find any air left in the room, but I dare not try too hard. I don't want Slither to remember that I'm there and shoot me too, so I sit like a fish thrown on the bank watching the fisherman work his bait.

He puts the gun in his back pocket and opens the door to the room. He has to step over Flat Top's body in order to do so but that doesn't seem to bother him at all. Slither grabs

Flat Top's bare foot and drags him in a circle so his toes are facing the door. Without a glance in my direction, he picks up both feet and drags his dead, faceless friend out the door, through the next room, and down the steps. The repetitive thud of Flat Top's head connecting with each step on the way down snaps me out of my shock. I follow the smear of blood out the door, past the fireplace with its mounted deer head— Slither's trophy of shame—and to the window overlooking the back yard. I don't go down the stairs. No reason to push my luck with a madman.

Slither drags Flat Top across the yard to the well, where he stops and drops the legs. I expect him to open the top of the well and drop him in, but he doesn't. He leaves him there. When Slither turns around, he glances up to the window. I'm not sure if he sees me, but I take no chances. I scramble back to the rape room.

There is nothing in this room I can use as a weapon. Maybe I could hit him with the lamp? Downstairs, I hear the door open and close. I listen without taking a breath, without moving a muscle.

Cupboard doors open and close, water sloshes. Is he making lunch? Like nothing even happened? But no, now he's climbing the stairs. I crawl back into bed. I've left the door between the rooms open, but there is no time to do anything about that. I'm sure he'll lock me in, or maybe he'll just shoot me.

When he reaches the top of the steps, I realize the sloshing noise came from the stock pot he's carrying. He's thrown a dishtowel over his shoulder, too.

"Here's some soapy water. You can wash yourself up. It's not warm, but it'll have to do." I notice that his hands are clean but there's blood smeared on his socks. He throws the dishcloth on the corner of the bed.

"I'm sorry if I scared you." His face is flat, his words monotone. He doesn't look at me.

"I'm gonna go make some soup. When you're done washing up, you can use the towel and water to clean up the blood on the floor."

"Okay," I say, but he doesn't wait for a response.

When he gets to the top of the stairs, he stops.

"Adam and Eve were naked in the garden before they ate the fruit. God approves of sex. Don't misunderstand my anger. There's nothing wrong with what you and I are doing here. Now wash up good. I'll be back later."

I do as he says. The water leaves me shivering, but the cool temperature feels good on my swollen parts. As quietly as I can, I search both bedrooms for my clothes but I can't find them, so I fashion a sort of toga with the bedsheet and scrub the blood off the floor.

Slither doesn't come back with food or drink for me. I haven't heard much movement in a while, so I think he might be napping. I could try to escape, but something tells me it's not the right time. I'm not ready.

Instead, I open the prayer book. One of my tarot cards falls out onto the floor.

The Seven of Wands.

This was one of the few good cards in my spread. The girl in the picture holds her wand up defensively against onslaught of six others.

Wands are power. Harness yours.

I remember how the old woman gripped my hand when she spoke. Her aged voice was soft but not at all frail. In my memory, it sounds like the voice of a woman's battle cry—steady and strong without need to be loud.

The prayer on the page marked by the card is not a prayer at all. It's a segment from Ovid's *Metamorphoses*:

The woods leapt away, a groan came from the ground, the bush blanched, the spattered sword was soaked with gouts of blood, stones brayed and bellowed, dogs began to bark, black snakes swarmed on the soil and ghostly shapes of silent Spirits floated through the air.

On the facing page is an illustration of The Magician—the old woman, with her hair down, blowing in a tempest. In this image, she has four hands. Two are conjuring a web that holds the Hanged Woman, as if she has control, but in her other hands she holds the cord and a pair of scissors. Beneath the illustration are the words: *Harness the power of your own magic; create the ending you desire. You have the power within you. The time has come.*

Within me. I must find my courage. I must stand and fight. There can be no backing down; there can be no pity.

You choose your cards, but you must also play them.

I close my eyes, and take a deep breath. In that breath, my body takes inventory of my wounds and weaknesses. Inside those breaks—where my enemy believes I am most vulnerable—I must place my weapons.

Gunshots knock me off my heroine's pedestal. Rushing to the butterfly window, I see my end taking shape.

It's over. My body responds as it did in my kitchen a million years ago—it turns to jelly. Slither stands between the house and the car, which now sits on four flat tires. The man has shot out each one.

My resolve has left me. The prayer book falls onto the floor beside me; my hand sweeps across the nightstand on my way down. I roll into a ball, vulnerable and thoughtless, waiting to give myself over to fate, for Slither to come in and take me to hell.

No. No, I'm not ready. I can't die now. Not after all I've already survived. I crab-crawl across the floor to the door and shut it as silently as possible. I check the window again. He's not out front anymore, but I haven't heard him come back inside either. I can't waste any more time.

There's enough space behind the bed that I can shove myself behind the headboard and push. It slides easily across the hardwood, but it makes a terrible screeching as it moves.

It doesn't matter anymore. This is war. I use it to barricade myself in the room—the room in which I've had my soul desecrated is now my only chance to save it.

Once again, I hold my breath and listen. My eyes scan the room for ideas on how to survive. The prayerbook is still open to The Magician. But she has abandoned me, cut the cord; I'm on my own now. She's even taken Black Dog with her.

For now, I will allow myself to cry. I collapse onto the bed and cry until my eyes burn so badly I can't open them. Sometime in this moment, I fall asleep.

X.

I am awakened by the slamming of a body against my door, and then a terrible scraping. Slither has discovered my barricade!

I open my eyes to find that it is deepest night. The bed is back in its original position. The scraping and pounding continues. I'm dreaming. I'm dreaming and Freddy Krueger is on the other side of the door with his finger-knives and blood lust. I must wake up.

I pinch myself on the way to the window, the one with the butterflies, but they aren't here anymore—everything has abandoned me. As I search for Charlotte's web, my eyes focus beyond the pane of glass to the moonlit yard where the car once stood.

The driveway is now a river. From this height, I can see bodies floating in it, motionless, faces locked in horror-filled screams. The old woman—the fortune teller, or is she The Magician?—sits beside the river. She is aware of me and turns her head, staring with those eyes, all-seeing yet blind, eyes that pull you inside their sickly white depths and hold you there with chaotic bands of scar tissue. In my dream, two have become six. She beckons me to come down to her with two of the four hands on her left side. The other two are busy with their counterparts washing bloodied garments in a sea of dead.

I am compelled to go to her, but I fear the beast beyond the door. I wish I could explain to the old spider woman that I am trapped, that I can't open that door and face what is on the other side.

Come. I hear her voice inside me. It thrums from within so that I feel not as if she has spoken to me, but that she has plucked one of my strings, tuning my soul. As the reverberation dies, I realize I am wrapped in silence. Her voice has quieted the thing beyond my room, and I am safe to depart.

The surface of the door has been gouged and shredded. My theory of an attack by a fictional horror movie killer could stand, that or a visit from the Bizarro World's Woody Woodpecker. The actual perpetrator, however, has left a calling card stuck in the wood of the door—a piece of antler embedded at door-knocker height. I pull it out to examine it.

This piece is two-pronged. One long, thin piece about four inches in length and the other branching from its base is much shorter but thicker with a length of only an inch or two. My warped brain thinks of the two different yet terrible appendages that invaded my privacy again and again—one long and thin, one short and girthy.

The buck who tried to ram open my door is gone from his usual perch above the mantle. In his haste, he has knocked over the clay pot and broken more of his antler off, which lies on the floor by the rug where once upon a time, a monster hid a gun for a frightened little girl. I vaguely remember her. She had a stuffed dog, didn't she? She liked dandelions and butterflies and had dreams of growing up to be a doctor. Was that it? What happened to her? She disappeared—locked away in a black room somewhere. *No time to consider all that now.* Instead, I take my gifts from the deer back to the bedroom and hide them under the pillow—offerings for some twisted tooth fairy.

On my way to the old spider woman, I stop at the back window to check on Flat Top. There must be a full moon because everything is perfectly illuminated—the snakes gliding over his legs, wriggling up and out of the crotch of his shorts likes some eldritch evil, and Black Dog! Black Dog hungrily devours what is left of Flat Top's face. My pet looks up, acknowledging my watchful stare with his bloodied muzzle and eyes the color of a harvest moon.

It is time for the reaping.

Downstairs, I tiptoe through the kitchen, careful not to bump into the table covered in empty beer bottles. Some of the bottles perch precariously on their sides, ready to roll off at the slightest nudge. I step on a bottle top and bite my lip, covering my mouth with my hand. This must be a dream, yet I will take no chances. I peek into the living room where Slither is passed out on the couch. *Good.* I notice one other thing as I exit—the refrigerator has been unplugged and shoved against the door to the black room. Is it possible that upstairs and outside is all a dream, but here on this floor with Slither, it is not? Perhaps, in this pink tower, reality shifts freely, as if life is just a poor television signal.

Come. My body hums with anticipation and anxiety. What does the old woman want to show me?

When I approach, I see that she has spun a long web. On it hang pink-tinged sheets and my bra. She must have gotten it from the car. She is washing a blood-soaked shirt in the river of the dead, smacking it against rocks and tearing it away from the clutches of desperate souls.

I watch, waiting to speak until spoken to. It seems that no matter what she does, the blood remains permanently affixed to the fibers of cloth.

Finally, when it seems as if she will never acknowledge me, I say, "Whose clothes are those?"

Without stopping or turning to me, she replies, "They are yours unless you do something to save yourself."

She works her gnarled hands into the shirt, shooing away the dead.

"We all suffer in this existence. Eventually, we walk the borderlands between life and death." As she says this, she points to the woods beyond the river, and then to the river itself. The dead breach the surface, stretching their arms out to grab at my ankles. I step back.

The old woman with six blind eyes and eight impossibly long arms continues. "When you reach the crossroads, which path will you choose? The forest is frightening and filled with uncertainties. The river flows ever on, absolute and predictable in its course and end."

"Is the river death?" I ask, but I know the answer. The answer is snatching at me, trying to pull me under. She hangs my shirt on the web beside my bra and jeans, which I didn't see before. The jeans are hanging upside down, my tarot cards spilled beneath them. I reach out for my clothes, suddenly aware and ashamed of my nakedness.

"Take what is yours," the old crone rasps.

I hesitate because my shirt and pants are dripping wet, but I take my cards, just as a rotted, decaying carcass that once was Flat Top flops up and out of the river, lunging for me.

The old spider woman knocks me away, causing me to drop most of my cards. "Go now! Wake up!"

And I do.

Day three

Sunday, June 28, 1992

THE DEVIL

7 OF WANDS

THE MAGICIAN

JUDGEMENT

XI.

It's early morning, and the old spider woman's words echo and snap like electricity in my waking ears. Confusion overwhelms my senses. The bed is against the door where I pushed it. Beneath my pillow, I find the double phallic antler along with the rest of the items from my dream. Butterflies have returned to the window; beyond them is not the underworld but a pillar of black smoke. Emanating from the smoke is the crackle of what I mistakenly thought was the old crone's voice, but I now realize is the car on fire. Slither has set the goddamned car on fire. He has no expectations of either of us ever leaving this place.

I hear Black Dog barking. He's back! But I don't want Slither to shoot him. Clearly, the man has murder/suicide on his agenda. I have to shoo him away, at least until I can come up with a plan. My door is unlocked and completely intact. No signs of a rogue beast or fictional slasher, yet the antler is real and still beneath my pillow. The mounted, taxidermized deer is gone. Either Slither took it down and broke a piece of antler off for me to find while I was sleeping, or my dream was more of a visit to the other side.

It seems like the answer should be clear, but here in my pink tower, it is not.

For instance, Black Dog is where I last saw him in my dream. I've come to think of him as my guide through this terror, so to watch him tear the purple, bloated flesh away from Flat Top's corpse is both satisfying and nauseating. Black Dog is not the only creature feasting on all that Flat Top's body has to offer. Several ravens are hopping about his ruined head. One of them has its beak buried deep into the cavity where Flat Top's unaffected eye once sat.

A large black snake is sunning itself on the corpse's shins. I'm mesmerized by this morbid life cycle revolving beneath me until Slither's shouts and curses shake me from my karmic soap opera. The birds scatter at his approach, and Black Dog barks.

"Please don't shoot him," I whisper, certain that is exactly what he is about to do. Instead, he shoots into the air and Black Dog runs away. Slither kicks the big snake off his one-time friend.

I expect him to finally dump the body into the well, but he doesn't; he just stands there. Twice he brings the gun up to his own temple, and I cheer him on.

"Pull the trigger. Just end this now." But again, he defies my expectations. As if he hears my thoughts, he looks up at me. We make eye contact, even with the distance between us. He lowers his head first.

It's time for me to stop reacting and save myself, follow the path the cards laid out for me—time to turn my wounds into weapons.

On the bed, back in the rape room, lies the only tarot card I managed to pull from my dream.

Judgment.

Judgment is the card of karma. It signals a change in consciousness—a cooperation with the spirit world. They have much to teach you. Judgment is the final lesson. It is time for Justice, time for Judgment, time for karma. The old woman's voice scratches at my brain.

In this room, I have the antlers gifted to me by the deer that once, like me, bore the brunt of Slither's inner turmoil, and my body. These are my tools.

Flat Top did not receive Justice. *A shot to the head was too good for him, and I hope he rots for all eternity in the old crone's river of the dead.*

Slither has pulled the Judgment card, he just doesn't know it yet. He had a chance to grow from his pain, to learn his cosmic lesson, and rise above, but he became like his enemy. I will not make that mistake. I will never become like them.

The old woman's cards gave me the key to my survival. I know what I must do now. There is no time to think anymore—only to act.

The pain is intense. My eyes water, and in the distance, Black Dog howls in commiseration. He is my mouthpiece. All the agony, the torment, the stings that I must hold inside, flow mournfully within his bays. When it is done, my hand is bloody and my body is sweaty. I could try to wipe it off but decide the stickiness of the blood may work to my advantage. For now, the larger part of the broken antler stays beneath my pillow. Black Dog settles down, and I wait as motionless as possible for the last of the tarot cards to be played.

When Slither comes into the room, he has the gun in his hand.

"You understand there's no way out of this. We both have to die," he says.

There is no emotion. I realize that all this time, his quiet, flat affect was not due to deep regret or shame. No, it was a sign of psychopathy. So, I will play to that; I bring up my shield.

"I understand. I think I always knew this would be how it ends." I look down shyly. "Can I have one last request, though? Just one thing before I die?"

He shifts his weight from one foot to the other, a crack in his veneer. "Maybe. What is it?"

I peer at him through my lashes, playing at the innocence he stole from me. "If I'm going to die at seventeen, can I please experience one sexual encounter that feels like love? Please? Will you do that for me? Can you make me feel loved? I don't want to be on my hands and knees. I want to look up and see love, or at least something resembling love, in the eyes of my partner. Can we do that?"

Tension relaxes his grip on the gun a bit. "You sure you want to do that?"

My voice trembles as I speak, but I find it is not due to fear. It is the current of power I hold within myself. "Yes. I'm sure. I know you were trying to make me feel good all along, but it just never felt right with two men. Maybe this would be better. Maybe I won't have to die so afraid."

For a moment, I swear I see a glimmer of sorrow flash across his face. He drops his gaze and bites his bottom lip. But then it's gone.

"Lie down, then."

I hope he doesn't notice the stiffness to my movements, the gingerly way I arrange myself. He's oblivious, too busy undressing. His dick is standing at attention. What kind of psycho can get an erection like that with the intent of shooting another human being and then himself in a matter of minutes?

As he crawls to me from the foot of the bed, I gently open my legs to receive him, hoping he doesn't try oral instead.

He doesn't. I keep my arms at my sides as he lies on top of me, kissing my neck, my chest, my nipples, before grabbing his dick in order to push it into me.

Only then do I bring my arms up to his neck as if I'm ready to embrace him. Just before he enters, I whisper, "Fuck me, Marty. I want you."

He responds the way I'd hoped.

Instead of a gentle slide into me, he thrusts hard. His eyes pop open wide and the scream that erupts from his body seems to come from every pore. His dick has been impaled by the antler I put in my vagina. I imagine the long, thin piece penetrating his urethra, and the smaller, shorter tip filleting his skin. He jerks his hips back, drawing his member with antler attached out of my body. It hurts me too, but I can't focus on that. Now is the time for the key to unlock my bondage. As he works frantically to detach the pointed horn of his trophy from his bloodied and ruined dick, I bring the second weapon out from under the pillow and anchor it between my palm and fingers. The dried blood keeps it from slipping as I stab him in the neck, burying at least three of the larger points. I think I hit near the carotid, so I withdraw it as I kick him off me, in the hopes that I've opened a vessel and blood will flow.

***

I reach the top of the stairs before Slither manages to get himself off the bed. He's trying to scream at me but it comes out garbled and gurgling. I realize that in my haste, I forgot to grab the gun off the nightstand. If he thinks of it I still may not make it out alive. As it is, managing the stairs with my shredded vagina is killing me. I block the screams it sends to my brain on nerve endings that run the length of my body, just as I have the last three days.

Somehow, he's right behind me when I reach the front door. I can't think about it. I hear him slip on the stairs. Maybe on my blood, maybe on his own? It buys me time to get the door open and myself outside. The heat from the still-smoldering car hits me in the face, and I choke on the fumes.

There's no choice; I have to change course to the backyard. I'll have to face Flat Top's mangled corpse. I hear Slither's gravelly breath as he tries to yell something, and I turn only to figure out how far away he is. His gun is raised at me, his chest covered in blood. I don't hear the gunshot though, only Black Dog's vicious snarl as he charges out of the woods and attacks Slither. I have time to see the blood spray when Black Dog's teeth make contact with Slither's already damaged throat before I go down, too. I feel like I got punched with a piece of rebar shot from a canon. There is a second of searing heat followed by an icy chill in my chest before all sensations are drowned out by a high pitch whining frequency that bores into my ears. Black Dog's fur becomes a cloud, expanding until it is all I see, and then I know nothing more.

XII.

Someone is whistling, trying to wake me up.

Whoo-stop-whoo-stop.

Black Dog is licking my face. I try to push him back but I can't seem to lift my left arm. I open my eyes to an inviting twilight that has shielded the harshness of the sun from my burning eyes and aching flesh. Taking inventory of my body, I find that my right arm is functioning well, I have to pee, and my left shoulder is smarting something fierce since I tried to move the arm attached to it. I push Black Dog away.

"Okay, boy. I'm okay. Stop." My voice is ancient, much older than the old woman's. In fact, it is like a dried husk of hers. It is in this attempt to speak that I discover the whistling is coming from me, from my chest. I reach for the hole thinking that I'll just plug it with my finger but the electric shock that accompanies my touch keeps me from trying further. Instead, I do my best to alleviate my full bladder. I need Black Dog's help in order to sit up. I hold tight to his neck and feel him stepping back, pulling me up. The blistering pain down below elicits a yelp from me.

Black Dog whines and nuzzles his nose close to my bullet wound. He's worried about me. He licks my face and runs off. I sit naked in the grass and let my bladder go. It burns—oh, how it burns—and tears come without permission.

I can't get up without my dog, so I wait. Soon, I hear him behind me. I turn my head as far as I can. Slither's blood-covered and decapitated corpse lies only about ten feet back. I don't want to look at him; instead, I see my dog, my familiar, the keeper of my soul, returning with a piece of sheet he has torn off the bed.

I do my best to tie my left arm tight against my shoulder, ensuring the material covers—and thereby muffles—my whistling wound. Black Dog helps me stand and remains motionless until the threat of unconsciousness ebbs away, and then he leads me into the backyard.

We pass what is left of Flat Top, which is mostly just smell. The woodland creatures have done a good job with clean up and disposal. There is a path in the forest, tarot cards strewn in a line like bread crumbs. Black Dog accompanies me past the threshold where lawn meets briars, and into the woods.

I stop, and, like Lot's wife, I cannot help but look back. One last look at the Pink Tower, my prison of three hundred-year days. Flat Top's and Slither's bodies float down the river of dead, which has returned. Their paths are certain and foreseen.

I've chosen the other path—unpredictable and uncharted. I know that soon enough, the path of cards will run out, that Black Dog will leave, and I'll be on my own. I hear traffic passing not too far ahead. I'm going to make it home.

I give Black Dog a scratch on the top of his head, between his ears.

"Thank you," I whisper. "I'm ready now."

The End.

EV KNIGHT is the author of the Bram Stoker Award-winning debut novel *The Fourth Whore*. She released her sophomore novel, *Children of Demeter*, as well as a novella, *Partum*, in 2021. EV lives in one of America's most haunted cities—Savannah, GA. When not out searching for the ghosts of the past, EV can be found at home with her husband Matt, her beloved Chinese Crested Gozer Augustus, and their three naughty sphynx cats—Feenix, Bizzabout Fitchett, and Ozymandias Fuzzfoot the First.

CREATURE PUBLISHING was founded on a passion for feminist discourse and horror's potential for social commentary and catharsis. Seeking to address the gender imbalance and lack of diversity traditionally found in the horror genre, Creature is a platform for stories which challenge the status quo. Our definition of feminist horror, broad and inclusive, expands the scope of what horror can be and who can make it.

CPSIA information can be obtained
at www.ICGtesting.com
Printed in the USA
BVHW072119240722
642920BV00002B/150

9 781951 971076